Standing in the gazebo was the figure of a man....

Eleanor blinked. Could it be...? No, this wasn't the ghost of her long-dead ancestor, the dashing Confederate Captain Wilding. Perhaps it was just a trick of the mist. Or maybe jet lag.

She shook her head. It *must* be the mist. After all, the Captain's ghost hadn't been sighted in years. And anyway, she didn't believe in ghosts anymore.

She stared at the motionless figure with a combination of fear and fascination, until the mist shifted, and the figure moved toward her. Goose bumps speckled the skin on her arms. What had once seemed incredibly romantic now seemed quite frightening.

He was only yards from her before she realized that the figure wasn't the gentle family ghost. It was something much worse.... It was Edan Bond.

KATHLEEN O'BRIEN, who lives in Florida, started out as a newspaper feature writer and television critic, but after marriage (to another journalist) and motherhood, she traded that in for the opportunity to work on a novel. Since then she's discovered how much she likes creating the perfect house for each story she writes. And Wildings—the antebellum home in *Between Mist and Midnight*—is no exception.

Books by Kathleen O'Brien

KATHLEEN O'BRIEN

Between Mist and Midnight

Harlequin Books

TORONTO • NEW YORK • LONDON
AMSTERDAM • PARIS • SYDNEY • HAMBURG
STOCKHOLM • ATHENS • TOKYO • MILAN
MADRID • WARSAW • BUDAPEST • AUCKLAND

To Manning, Irene and Michael, with all my love

Harlequin Presents first edition December 1992
ISBN 0-373-11515-6

BETWEEN MIST AND MIDNIGHT

CHAPTER ONE

MIDSTRIDE, MIDBREATH, Eleanor Wilding froze. The
evening mist swirled, tumbling backward against her,
as if confused by her sudden halt. Her suitcases fell
from her weakened hands, crushing the wisteria blossoms that littered the path. She heard herself gasp, and
the breath had words in it. No. It couldn't be....

An owl called an echoing question into the night, and
fear skimmed across her skin, prickling as it went.
Ahead of her the gazebo floated in the mist like a spectral ship festooned with cobwebs. And standing in the
gazebo was the figure of a man.

Her heartbeat was loud in the evening silence. She
blinked hard. Who could it be? No one should be at
Wildings tonight, no one but her grandmother, whose
petite figure certainly didn't resemble a man's and who,
at eighty-six, was hardly likely to be outdoors alone at
night.

So, who? Eleanor had arrived a day early; the rest of
the family wouldn't come until tomorrow. She blinked
again. Perhaps it was just a trick of the mist. Maybe jet
lag? She was tired. Otherwise such a foolish thought
would never have occurred to her.

She shook her head slightly, currents of wet Mississippi spring air slipping across her cheeks. It *must* be the
mist. The ghost of the long-dead Jonathan Wilding,
brave captain of the Confederacy, hadn't been sighted

on the riverbanks of Wildings in years. She'd been the last to "see" it, and that had been ten years ago. She didn't believe in ghosts anymore.

Her lungs hurt, and she realized she wasn't breathing. The odor of the smashed wisteria pressed against her nostrils, forcing her to inhale its sickly sweetness. Strange how clearly she remembered the captain. She'd been only fifteen when she'd seen him. Correction— *thought* she'd seen him, thought he was watching her as she wept in the moonlight, sending waves of sympathy to the child who'd felt so friendless. Funny the tricks tears and abject loneliness could play.

Ridiculous. And yet the shape in the gazebo tonight might have been conjured up straight out of her dreams—soft Confederate gray on a lean, military-straight body, staring out toward the bayou, one hand hooked onto the lattice of the gazebo. It projected the same sense of isolation, of longing, that had made her feel so akin to the ghostly captain.

She stared at the motionless figure with the combination of fear and fascination she'd always experienced, then remembered how her cousins had laughed at her tales. Especially her father's stepson, Edan Bond. He had teased her mercilessly. "Ghosts, Nell? Uh-oh. Don't tell me you've inherited the legendary Wilding madness."

She'd kicked him then, infuriated. There were no legends of madness in the Wilding family, and he shouldn't say such a thing. He wasn't even a Wilding. He was an interloper, an outsider. So what if, a year after her parents' divorce, her father had married Edan's mother and doted disgustingly on his new stepson? That inexplicable fondness was the only sign of madness in the Wilding family *she* had ever heard of.

How could anyone love Edan Bond? She had kicked him again, twice—once because she hated him and once because her father loved him.

The wisteria rustled as a small breeze slithered through it, and a long strand of her blond hair draped itself across her lips. The air around the gazebo swirled, too, and the mist shifted, forming new patterns around the tall figure.

When he turned, she almost cried out. Goose bumps speckled the skin on her arms. What had seemed romantic to her as a child suddenly seemed quite frightening. And yet it didn't occur to her to run. She waited, as though paralyzed, while the mist parted, and the figure moved toward her.

The light was so poor that he was only yards from her before she realized that the gray he wore was actually a suede jacket over charcoal corduroy slacks, not a bit like a confederate uniform, really. And that face...

Her heart beat in a slow painful rhythm. Not her gentle ghost, then. Something much worse. Edan Bond. What was Edan Bond doing here?

"Hi, Nell." As he spoke, a familiar resentment tightened her midsection. He had no business calling her Nell. No one had ever called her Nell except her father. Edan did it just to annoy her. "It's been a long time."

Swallowing hard, she fought the temptation to counter with an adolescent *Not long enough*.

"Edan." Her voice lacked any hint of welcome, and she dragged the stray hair from her lips without smiling. She tried to breathe evenly. What a field day he'd have if he knew she'd mistaken him for the ghost! "What are you doing here?"

A lazy grin stretched his generous mouth, tilting the corners of his deep-set eyes, but she clamped down firmly on the instinctive skitter of appreciation that disrupted her pulse. Oh, yes, he was handsome. She'd never denied that. But while her teenage cousins had swooned over him, she'd simply pronounced his looks "too surface." She wasn't sure what that meant, but it had sounded like a sophisticated put-down, and she'd hoped it would effectively hide her real feelings.

He had grown even more good-looking. Five years had elapsed since their last meeting and now, at twenty-nine, he was truly a man, all trace of immaturity erased. His wavy black hair—which had tickled his neck and ears during his college days—was clipped short, exposing the hard outlines of his face, from the pronounced angles where his jaw met his neck to the powerful ridge where his high cheekbones rose toward his temples. His gray eyes were a shade somewhere between mist and midnight, fringed by thick black lashes so long they might, on another man, have been girlish. But not on Edan. He was too tall, too broad in the shoulders, for there to be any confusion about his masculinity.

"What am I doing here? Same thing you are, I suppose." He was looking her up and down, apparently not finding her as improved as she found him. "I'm here for the reunion."

"But..." Ignoring the quick flash of anger she felt, she arranged her face in polite surprise. Her grandmother hadn't mentioned inviting Edan, probably knowing that Eleanor wouldn't have come if she'd thought he'd be here.

"But I thought this was a—" she pretended to be delicately searching for the right word "—*family* reunion."

His dark brows twitched together, and his strong jaw became subtly stronger in the moonlight. Obviously the barb had connected, but his voice betrayed nothing.

"I guess Charlotte is using the word loosely. She seems willing to include those of us who are connected by affection rather than by blood—like me—as well as those who are connected by blood rather than by affection." His smile grew nastier. "Like you."

Well, she'd asked for it. The first words out of her mouth had been combative. Being around Edan brought out the worst in her. Already she felt a small blush of shame in her cheeks. She had hoped she was past all this. She drew in a breath, ready to apologize, but, before she could speak, his voice roughened.

"How long has it been since you've visited Charlotte, Nell? How many years?"

"Five." Her lips were stiff as she tried to control her annoyance. She musn't let him upset her so easily. Surely she'd outgrown that. But he knew perfectly well how long it had been. No one, not even the self-centered Edan Bond, could have forgotten their last meeting.

The ugly pictures were forever etched in her mind. Five years ago, at her father's funeral. And, later that dreadful afternoon, at the reading of the will. How angry she'd been at him! And it wasn't because of the will, which had left him control of everything. It was because, by not telling her about her father's heart condition, he had robbed her of something that meant much more than money—the chance to say goodbye.

"Five years." His tone clearly communicated what he thought of that. Without further comment he slid his hands out of his pockets and reached over to pick up her suitcases. The muscles under his silver-gray suede jacket bulged as he hoisted the heavy bags.

"You'll have to let me show you around, then," he said, his voice returning to its earlier casual sarcasm. It was the tone he had always used with her, the superior, amused, barely tolerant tone that had constantly infuriated her. "A lot has changed."

Without waiting for her acquiescence, he moved up the wisteria-lined path toward the house, the mist forming a restless aura around him.

She followed almost helplessly, staring at his back, frustration hot in her chest. How like Edan, taking charge, leading the way, making *her* feel like the outsider. He had done it from the first day she'd met him, ten years ago, and he was doing it still. Her cheeks burned.

"See where we had to cut down the old oak—the one we used to climb?" He pointed, but she didn't look. She knew exactly which tree he meant.

"Borer beetles got it," he said, brushing past a dangling cluster of wisteria, triggering an explosion of scent.

A few overripe blossoms jiggled loose and rained onto his shoulder. He had always had the broadest shoulders. The cousins used to declare themselves positively faint whenever he appeared shirtless. Eleanor had a sudden flash of memory, more physical than mental, of those thick muscles under her trembling hands. Her palms tingled disagreeably. She clenched her fists, digging her nails into the skin, and she felt angrier than ever.

"Pity," she managed. "It was a beautiful tree."

"Mmm." He'd lost interest in the tree. "We decided to put in a new floor on the back porch, too. Wood finally rotted through."

She bit her lower lip, holding back her feelings of resentment. *We had to . . . we decided . . .* She knew from Charlotte's letters that he didn't actually live at Wildings anymore, but he certainly had a proprietary air. She realized suddenly that she resented his . . . *belonging* most of all. When her parents had divorced ten years ago, she hadn't been allowed to live at Wildings, except during summers and the odd holiday. She'd been sent first to her stepfather's home in Louisiana and then, a year later, to a boarding school. Miserable, she had run away at eighteen to make her own life in California. Since then she'd come back just once—for her father's funeral.

But somehow even knowing that her exile had been self-imposed didn't help. It still hurt to see Edan, the favored son, strolling through the gardens she had been able to visit only in her dreams.

Preoccupied by her bitter thoughts, she was caught unawares when, at the end of the trellis, he stopped abruptly and turned. She skidded to a halt but couldn't avoid stumbling into him, balancing herself with open palms against the soft suede of his jacket.

"What? What's the matter?" she asked irritably to cover her confusion as she pulled back.

"A warning. It's not just the house that's feeling the years," he said, his voice strangely harsh in the sweet air. "It's Charlotte, too. You're going to be surprised at how frail she looks. You mustn't show it. And she doesn't have much stamina, especially this late at night. I'll take you up, but you mustn't tire her."

"I won't," she said, his lord-of-the-manor tone finally igniting her banked anger. You'd think she was some traveling salesman, pestering the royal Wildings.

"I'm not a fool, Edan. I don't need you to instruct me on how to treat my own grandmother."

She knew her blue eyes were flashing and wished she could control her temper. What regression! She'd spent ten years trying to get her feelings for Edan into perspective. She was a grown woman now, not a spoiled and angry little girl. Why was she acting like one? "And I certainly don't need you to take me up. I have my own key—unless you've changed the locks along with everything else."

He raised one arched brow, a trick that had always annoyed her. Hours spent in front of her bedroom mirror attempting to copy it had been in vain. "No," he said coolly. "We didn't change the locks."

"Good. Then I think I'll go up alone. This is my family's house, remember? *I'm* a Wilding, in case you've forgotten."

The suitcases dropped from his hands. "No. I haven't forgotten. But I wondered if *you* had, since you haven't bothered to show your pretty pout around here in five years." He curled his lips. "Not that it hasn't been quieter without you—but Charlotte's been pining for you. Would it have killed you to come just once in all those years?"

"I couldn't." And she couldn't explain it to him. Besides, why should she? She set her mouth, though she knew it made her look like a little girl—a bad-tempered little girl. "But it really isn't any of your business, is it?"

"Why?" He clipped the word. "Because I'm not a Wilding? It's funny—in the five years you've been gone no one has felt it necessary to remind me of that. You've done it twice in five minutes."

She tilted her chin and met his eyes. They were dark now, definitely midnight, and although his tone was light, she knew he was angry. Still under control, though, not in a rage, thank heaven. She was all too aware of how Edan looked in a rage, and she never wanted to see that again.

"Anyway, it *is* my business," he continued. "It's my business because I care about Charlotte." A softness entered his expression, but Eleanor knew it wasn't for her. "She's been good to me."

"Oh?" Eleanor's eyes narrowed. It was true; her grandmother had always welcomed Edan Bond warmly to Wildings, as if he had been a real grandson. Just as her father had treated him like a real son, leaving him everything.

Words she hadn't ever meant to speak came marching out, as though they'd been waiting for the call to arms. "And maybe you're hoping she'll be better still, perhaps even remember you in her will?"

Instantly she knew she had gone too far. That was downright ugly, and it was beneath her. She wanted to say she was sorry, but didn't know how. A pulse throbbed in his temple, just behind the dark feathered curls at his hairline. A sound too low to be an oath gunned past his lips as he grabbed her shoulders.

"You haven't changed at all, have you? You're still a spiteful little girl, peeved because you're not getting all the attention."

"Well, am I wrong?" she asked defiantly, refusing to let his cold gray eyes intimidate her. She didn't want to apologize anymore. His insult hurt; it hit home too accurately. "You neatly managed to get control of my father's business when he died. Why stop now? Why not try to get Wildings, too?"

He shook her shoulders—just once, but hard enough to whip her hair against her neck and force her teeth together sharply.

"Why, you little—" He bit off whatever words had been about to follow. The tension in his strong hands told her he would have liked to shake her again, more thoroughly, but he restrained himself. "Your father left his company in my hands because I worked my tail off for him, and you know it. Nothing gets handed to you on a platter simply because you're a Wilding, sweetheart. You've got to give love and loyalty to get any."

His grip relaxed, as though he had surprised even himself with his vehemence. He stared at her a long moment, then released her with a slight shove.

"But why am I bothering? You don't even know what I'm talking about. You've never loved anybody but yourself, have you, Nell?"

He waited with one quirked eyebrow, his face patterned by the lacy shadows of wisteria. "Hmm?"

She wanted to toss back a saucy retort, but suddenly she couldn't. She gazed at him mutely, dumbstruck by the tumult of emotions that stormed through her heart. Her bitterness gave way to a confused misery, and she felt more like a child than a grown woman. It was so unfair. It had always been so unfair.

Never loved anybody? Of course she had, a plaintive voice inside her cried. She had loved and loved and loved until she was sick with loving. But no one had ever loved her back. Not her pretty mother, always busy with her second husband. Not her father, who—because she was a useless girl—had only wanted her out of the way. And certainly not Edan Bond, to whom she had given the only passion she'd ever known, and who had broken her heart.

But if she thought the years they'd been apart might have softened him toward her, she was mistaken. After five minutes, she saw that they were right where they'd left off. Enemies. Blinking back the threat of tears, she swallowed the rocky lump in her throat.

"I'm sure I'd find your lecture on love quite enlightening," she said, "but it's getting late, and I want to see my grandmother."

She bent to retrieve the suitcases, but his strong hands stopped her, clamping down over hers.

"You didn't answer my question, Eleanor." He pulled her up straight, so that their eyes locked. "Did you?"

"Did I what?"

"Learn to love anybody. It's been five years. That should have been long enough, even for you." He twisted her arm gently but firmly, until it was behind her. The motion edged her toward him, until their legs brushed together. She tilted her head back, trying to keep her distance without looking obvious. But he tugged her closer, until her breasts grazed his chest.

"Did you fall in love out there in California?"

She shivered, as if the clammy mist had been trapped between their bodies and, seeking an outlet, made its way through her clothes into her skin. With his hand still locked on hers behind her back, he pressed it against the base of her spine, nudging her for an answer. It clearly wasn't intended as a seductive gesture. His face held that too-familiar mixture of amusement and contempt.

"Well?"

She mustn't shut her eyes. Even though the shivering went all the way up to her cheekbones, she mustn't shut her eyes. In spite of his casual disdain, it would be far too easy to drift back into wanting him, down into the hopeless pit of need that had sent her running from Wildings in the first place. He was so sensual, so full of masculinity and power....

No. Better to remember how much she hated him.

"No," she said, her eyes steady on his. She blinked to clear her vision. "No, I didn't fall in love."

His eyes were unreadable. "Oh? Why not?" His hand pushed again, and the combined heat of their fingers steamed into her. "Let's see . . . you wouldn't be carrying a torch for a certain Southern gentleman, would you?"

Her face froze. "What?"

"A certain Confederate captain, perhaps?" Now his expression was easily read. He was taking a malicious delight in tormenting her. "I seem to recall you had a definite fondness for the ethereal type."

When he smiled like that he reminded her of the old Edan, the cocky teenager who had laughed at her fantasies, ganging up with her cousins to make her look foolish. Well, she was an adult now, and he couldn't get away with that anymore.

She wrenched herself free and grabbed her suitcases.

"I guess I was just looking for a real man," she said, her voice all sugar over acid. "And a hundred-year-old ghost came closer than anyone else around here."

If she had expected that taunt to hurt, she was destined to be disappointed. He threw back his head and laughed, teeth sparking in the moonlight.

He was still laughing when she opened the front door of Wildings. It required enormous self-restraint not to slam it in his face.

HER GRANDMOTHER was asleep.

A fire that had almost burned out crackled low in the grate. Charlotte sat in the Queen Anne armchair, book upside down on her lap quilt and her head back against the wing at a delicate tilt. Her blue eyes, those big eyes that Eleanor had inherited, were closed, and her prim pinkened mouth was slightly slack.

Eleanor stopped in the doorway, suddenly thankful that Charlotte couldn't see her. Could she have hidden her shock? No wonder Edan had thought it necessary to warn her.

Her grandmother had never been a big woman. "Don't fret about it, Eleanor," she had always said. "What Wilding women lack in stature we make up in sheer ferocity." But tonight the woman in the chair appeared wraithlike. She must have lost twenty pounds, Eleanor thought with a sinking sensation. Her soft pink shirtwaist dress looked two sizes too big and her curly white hair, the one thing about her that was completely undiminished, framed a small, frighteningly pale face.

A rush of helpless love flooded over Eleanor as she stood watching the old woman sleep. Such a little body to hold such a strong spirit! Somehow she knew, if only from the meticulous grooming and the elegant angle of her grandmother's sleeping head, that the spirit had kept its strength even though the body faltered.

Eleanor smiled, and the smile had tears in it. In spite of Edan Bond, Wildings still felt like home. It was the only place in the world that ever had. So many nights during her troubled childhood she had sat in this room, by just such a dwindling fire, taking comfort from her grandmother's wisdom, her tart and accurate evaluation of people and problems. Eleanor swallowed. Thank goodness she'd come back in time.

"Edan? Is she here yet?"

Charlotte leaned forward, her fine-boned veined hands clutching the book that threatened to slip off her lap.

Hidden in the shadows of the doorway, Eleanor swallowed again, trying to push down the emotion that had overwhelmed her. Before she could collect herself, a deep voice at her shoulder answered.

"Yes, Charlotte. She's here."

Eleanor cast a quick glance of irritated surprise at Edan. How long had he been standing there? Hadn't she made it clear she wanted to come up alone? She moved in to greet her grandmother.

"Hi, Gran, darling," she said, careful to erase all signs of worry from her face with a wide smile. She enveloped the tiny body in a warm embrace. "Oh, Gran, I've missed you so."

"Well, of course you have." Charlotte's hug was not as strong as Eleanor remembered it, but her voice was as saucy as ever. "You've been gone for five years."

The words had no bite, no implied criticism, but tears stung Eleanor's eyelids, anyway. "I know," she whispered against her grandmother's neck. "I'm sorry."

"Nonsense." Charlotte said, bringing her thin hands around to Eleanor's shoulders. "You've been busy. Busy growing up. Now, let me look at you. Let's see if five years in California made one of those impossible Valley Girls out of you."

Eleanor straightened up for inspection. "Not a chance, Gran," she said with a smile. "I wouldn't have dared."

"Well, you never know." Charlotte sniffed, but her eyes held a sparkle. "My influence might not have stretched across the whole continent."

"To the moon, Gran." Eleanor laughed out loud. "And back again. I'll be hearing your edicts, which all began with 'Wilding women never...' as long as I live."

Charlotte chuckled and, taking Eleanor's hands, held them wide apart for a better survey. She twirled her granddaughter slowly.

"You *are* different, though," Charlotte declared finally. She fingered the soft yellow wool of Eleanor's skirt. "Isn't she, Edan? She can't climb trees in this. Where's my little tomboy?"

Eleanor blushed, her eyes flicking to the doorway, where Edan still stood, watching. His eyes leisurely scanned her, a faked surprise on his lips, as though he hadn't noticed any change until this very moment. After taking in the full skirt and clinging, buttery yellow sweater, his gaze lingered on the ecru lace at her throat and the blond hair that had been allowed to grow very long. Then he turned to Charlotte.

"Quite a new person," he said. "This may be the first time I've ever seen her without a scrape on her knee."

Eleanor's cheeks burned, and she pressed her lips together to keep her annoyance from taking verbal form. The fact that his statement was probably true didn't help. She *had* always been scraped and bruised, and they both knew why. She'd been pathetic in her need to outride Edan on horseback, to outrun him in the fields, to outscore him at baseball, to outclimb him in the oak trees. She'd yanked her hair back into an unbecoming ponytail, donned cutoffs and proceeded to bruise every inch of her developing body in an effort to show her father that a daughter could be just as good as a stepson.

Edan would always be so mocking, raising one eyebrow as she came sliding into home a split second after the pitcher had thrown her out. "You don't make much of a boy, do you, Nell?" And he would let his eyes roam down her clay-covered jersey. "But then you don't make much of a girl, either."

All that derision. All that dirt. All those bloody knees and aching arms. And her father hadn't even noticed.

Now Edan met the flash in her eyes with an amused smirk.

"But we'll take care of that this weekend, won't we, Charlotte? Don't you have one of your annual Wilding free-for-alls planned? That should put a few scrapes back on those knees. Unless, of course, Nell is too prim to play these days."

Charlotte chuckled. "He means the softball game, Eleanor. You probably remember it sometimes gets out of hand."

"I remember." Eleanor met Edan's gaze without blinking and pasted on a smile she felt sure he'd recognize as phony. "I can hardly wait. I hope you've been practicing, Edan. Out in L.A. I pitch for the center's team. Three no-hitters last season."

He grinned back. "I'm impressed," he said, looking anything but. "Don't count on having any of those here," he added. "It's pretty hard to strike *me* out."

Eleanor's eyes narrowed, but Charlotte's broke in, still chuckling.

"Oh, off with you, Edan. You two can go at each other all you like tomorrow. Tonight I want to have some long girl-talk with my granddaughter."

Edan hesitated, but Charlotte fluttered her hand, impatiently waving him toward the door.

"Scoot," she said. "Why don't you call your mother? I talked to her a little while ago, and I think she's homesick. It's still early on the West Coast, and she's sitting in her hotel room.''

"Oh. Isn't she coming for the reunion?" Eleanor was disappointed. Edan's mother had always been kind to her in spite of everything. "I'm sorry to hear that."

Edan's face showed how little he believed her, but Charlotte didn't give him time to voice his skepticism.

"Yes, it's too bad." Charlotte agreed. "But she had a chance for a lovely vacation, and she couldn't pass it up." She frowned at Edan. "Now be a good son and call her. You're in the way here."

To Eleanor's surprise, Edan took his dismissal in good grace.

"Okay, boss," he said, leaning over to give Charlotte a kiss on the cheek. "But don't stay up too late."

She patted his cheek smartly. "I'll stay up as long as I want," she retorted. "I plan to stay up until I hear every single one of Eleanor's juicy stories. If you're tired, *you* go to bed."

Edan laughed, but at the door he turned back to send a grim look Eleanor's way. He nodded at the clock over the fireplace as if reminding her of the time.

She simply stared, deliberately uncomprehending. Her grandmother had dismissed him, and he had no right to boss either of them around. If she'd been fifteen again, she would have stuck out her tongue at him.

"Good night, Edan," she called sweetly.

His answer was ominous. "And tomorrow," he said, "*we'll* talk."

CHAPTER TWO

AS THE BANJO CLOCK in the front parlor chimed twice, Eleanor made her way down the dark staircase, walking on the balls of her bare feet so that her weight wouldn't disturb the old wood too much. Without thinking, she skipped the fifth stair and then smiled at herself. The telltale stair, Edan had called it—the one that exposed guilty teenagers sneaking up after curfew, hungry kids creeping down to snitch the last piece of pie, and once even a clumsy burglar trying to make off with the silver service.

She managed to reach the kitchen without incident and, leaving the overhead lights untouched, clicked on the small bulb above the stove. The last thing she needed was Edan waking up and coming to check on her. She'd be ready to face him tomorrow, she promised herself. Tonight too many ghosts haunted Wildings. Not the lonely captain; he was tame compared to the ghosts that visited her now, the yearning, angry ghosts of her younger self. No wonder she couldn't sleep.

She heated a pan of milk on the front burner, ignoring the microwave oven that would have been so much quicker. She instinctively sought the rituals of her childhood, as though licking milk from a warm wooden spoon would keep sad memories at bay.

It did help, a little. Carrying the mug of milk to the breakfast nook, she plopped down on the chair closest to the window. Moonlight fractured by oak branches dappled her arms as, hunching forward, she stared out into the thickening mist. She could barely make out the gazebo, a denser patch of white in the filmy distance.

Frowning, she sipped from the steaming mug. She hadn't remembered that you could see the gazebo from here. She'd always felt so isolated out there, almost in another world. And surely the night that she and Edan...

Her brow cleared. No. You hadn't been able to see the gazebo then. It had been hidden by the big oak tree they used to climb, and now the tree was gone.

The girl who had been out at the gazebo that night was gone, too. Absently her fingers caressed the underside of the old wooden table, searching until they came to the roughened grooves she knew so well. She followed the curves with her fingertips. EB. Crude letters, scratched into the wood with the tine of her fork while she should have been eating her pancakes. It was the only place she had ever admitted the truth. EB. Even there she hadn't dared to write the rest of it: EW loves EB.

She pulled her fingers away and pressed them against her closed eyelids, trying to shut out the gazebo, the table, the whole painful mess. But the memories continued to present themselves. They had lived inside her for nearly nine years. There was no way to escape them.

It had been so stupid. Now, after getting her degree in psychology, she knew enough to recognize the hidden motivations at work when she'd left that foolish note under Edan's pillow. Back then, at just-turned-sixteen, she hadn't had an inkling.

It was supposed to have been a practical joke designed merely to annoy him. She'd cooked up the idea with one of her best friends, and they'd giggled over the typewriter for hours, devising the perfect plan. Late that night Eleanor had slipped a pink perfumed note under Edan's pillow. *Meet me at the gazebo at midnight—N.*

It would be too funny. Edan's current girlfriend was Nancy, a buxom blond classmate he'd brought home from college for spring vacation. Eleanor and her friend decided that the disgustingly well-endowed Nancy definitely looked the type for midnight trysts. How silly Edan would feel, all primed for romance only to find out he'd been snookered! And the note wasn't even an outright lie. After all, Nell began with an *N*, too.

There wasn't any moon that night. During the daytime the azalea bushes were a conflagration of red, orange and pink, but at midnight they were only strange blue-black blossoms against black leaves.

As she picked her way down to the gazebo, her thin bedroom slippers allowing every stone and twig to bruise her feet, she felt her first twinge of regret. Maybe the joke was dumb. Maybe she should go back to the house. . . .

But she kept walking, refusing to give up, though it was hard to see where she was going, and worse, it was much colder than she'd bargained for. Gratefully she reached the small latticed gazebo and waited there, gathering her robe close around her throat—glad that it had a hood—hoping he wouldn't be late.

He wasn't.

While she stared out toward the water, he slipped up behind her as silently as a ghost. She didn't hear him, didn't sense him. She knew only that strong hands abruptly slid up under her arms and across her rib cage, pressing her backward until she met a hard-muscled chest.

"Hi," he whispered into her hood. He kissed her neck through the robe. "It's kind of cold for this, don't you think?"

She couldn't speak. The embrace had been so unexpected there had been no time for indignation. An unfamiliar heat flooded her, drowning speech.

"Hey." He nuzzled her neck again, sending goose bumps up the back of her scalp. "We'd better go in. Aren't you cold?"

Still she didn't answer. She knew he wasn't really talking to her. He thought she was Nancy; that was the only reason he was touching her. If she could have worked a miracle at that moment she would have *become* Nancy. She suddenly wanted nothing more but for him to go on touching her.

His fingers moved upward, his thumbs teasing at the rounded sides of her breasts, tantalizingly skimming their edges. No one had ever touched her this way before, and she was nearly sick with the thrill of it.

His hands roamed lazily across the flat plane of her stomach, making small intense circles that seemed to spiral down into the very core of her. She felt herself melting. How was he doing this to her? It was as though his hands spoke to her body, as though they mutely told her muscles to tighten, her blood to scald, her breath to quicken. His lips were speaking, too, using kisses instead of words to ignite tiny stinging fires at the nape of her neck, at the pulse of her throat, at the unprotected curve of her ear.

Streaks of hot lightning spread through her, hardening her nipples and weakening her knees. Her breath misted the cold air, and her head fell back against his shoulder.

Don't stop, the accelerating beat of her heart seemed to be saying over and over, faster and faster. She had sometimes thought about Edan this way, wondering what he and his girlfriends did when they were alone, but she had never imagined that it felt like this. This wasn't something to giggle or snicker about. This was as profound, as frightening, as dying. Or as thrilling as being born.

"Come on, Nance. It's late. Let's go in."

How could he sound so casual? His breathing was even. His hands were now quiescent, seeming to have no interest in further exploration. They were cool, as if the blaze that raged through her hadn't touched him at all. How could that be? Could he really go back inside now and forget this had ever happened?

Well, she couldn't. She needed more. She wanted him to know whose body it was that he'd inflamed this way. She wanted him to care.

"Edan," she whispered, catching his hands with her own trembling ones. "Edan, it's me. It's Eleanor."

She heard his horrified intake of breath, felt the rocklike paralysis that froze his hands.

"Nell?" His lips were still against her neck. "Oh, Lord, no. Nell?"

"Yes," she answered, not turning her face to his. She couldn't bear to see disappointment there. She rubbed her cheek against his chin and stroked his thumbs desperately. "But it's okay, Edan. It's okay."

He jerked, trying to pull away, but she refused to relinquish his hands. She pressed them against her rib cage, where they rose and fell with her labored breathing.

"Don't stop," she begged, pushing harder, as though she could meld him to her. "I want you—"

He pulled again, roughly. "Nellie, no."

"Yes." Tears stung her eyes. She was losing him. He didn't want her. Frantically she clutched his hands, dragging them up to her breasts. Her heart fluttered beneath his fingers, and her breasts swelled under his touch. "Oh, please, Edan. I want you to."

He moaned, a low animal sound, and dropped his face into the velvet folds of her robed shoulder. His fingers tightened, and he exhaled a deep shuddering breath. Slowly, infinitesimally, as though they did so without his permission, his hands slid across her tender breasts. Her nipples, tight and sensitive, rubbed against his palms.

Fire exploded from an aching spot between her legs and raced up to the places where he held her. She didn't think she could stand; she leaned back to let his strength support her.

His body was hard against her, and masculine in a way she only dimly understood. It seemed to strain toward an answering femininity in her.

"I want you," she said, pressing against him, spooning her body into his in a shameless desire to know every inch of him. Her head had fallen against his shoulder, and she spoke the words to the starless sky. "I want you to make love to me."

For one triumphant terrifying moment she thought he would obey her. In his hands she felt the fire she had been seeking earlier. And in the wordless groan that vibrated against her ear she heard a need as fierce as her own.

"*No!*" He tore his hands away and stumbled back, blindly encountering the gazebo wall.

"Damn you, Eleanor," he said, his voice harsh. "What the hell are you trying to do? This is a dangerous game."

She couldn't see his face clearly, only the glitter of his eyes in the black night. But his voice was cruel, and it made her desperate. She needed his hands again.

She moved toward him, fighting her tears. "What do you mean, a game?" She put her hands on his chest. His heart was throbbing violently, and she massaged him with her fingers, reaching under his sweater to feel his smooth, slick skin. Even on this cold night he was perspiring. "Don't you want me?"

He squeezed his eyes shut as her hands traveled the length of his chest, down toward his belt and up again. "No. Stop it, Nellie. I don't."

But his heart kept racing under her hands. She probed with her fingers and found the hardened nubs of his nipples. Instinctively she rubbed them with her thumbs, remembering how her own had felt. Was he feeling it, too?

"Stop!" He grabbed her wrists convulsively, pulling her hands away and imprisoning them just inches from his body. She could not reach him.

"Why?" She heard the begging note in her voice, but she couldn't help herself. "You would if I were Nancy, wouldn't you?" Her voice broke as she remembered how different Nancy's voluptuous body was from hers. Eleanor's legs were coltish, her hips still narrow. And her breasts—her cheeks flushed at the thought—her breasts were round and high and firm, with none of the feminine jiggle that men seemed to love so much.

"Is it me . . . my body?" She couldn't believe she was asking. Was it possible that desire could overcome all pride, all shame? "I'm not pretty enough? I know I'm not . . . like Nancy, but—" She broke off miserably.

"Shut up, Nell." His hands tightened on her wrists. "That's a damned stupid question, and you know it."

"I do not!" Why did he sound so angry? She managed to lift one hand and brush his lower lip. It was hot.

"How could I know?" A small sob escaped her. Her wrists hurt where he held them. "I want you to touch me, but you won't, and I don't know if I just don't . . . don't please you. . . ."

He made a sound like a groan. "How could you not know?" His eyes glittered into hers with a strange brightness. Their gaze held, but slowly his arm moved, forcing her left hand down between them. It grazed the waistband of his jeans. Panicking, she resisted, but he pressed harder until her trembling fingers touched the rigid length of his manhood.

"There, damn you," he said, so tightly that it seemed his mouth didn't move. "You're not so young that you don't know what that means, are you? Now tell me that you think your body doesn't please me."

She shook her head numbly. She knew. She didn't know exactly how she knew, but she was quite sure it meant he wanted her as painfully as she wanted him. Her fingers pressed against the hardness.

"Oh, Edan," she murmured, a strange exultation making her head light. "Oh, Edan."

"*That's* why I say it's not a game. Make love to you? You don't even know what that means. Damn it, you're only a kid. You don't know what you're doing to me."

"Then show me," she whispered, running her fingers along the length of him, marveling that he seemed to grow larger under her touch. "I want to know."

She could almost hear the tension around them crack. A guttural cry escaped him, and he yanked her against him. Her hand was trapped between their bodies.

"Damn you," he muttered hoarsely. "Damn you for looking like this, for feeling like this." His hands rose roughly up her body, stopping at the swell of her breasts. "This should never have happened. I swore it would never happen."

But she heard the unleashed need in his voice, and she knew it *would* happen.

Yes, the blood pounded in her ears. Yes and yes and yes.

There was no time for tenderness. It was as if demons drove him, as if he couldn't allow himself time to think, time to come to his senses. He tore at the snaps of her robe, growling when they resisted, until she was completely open to him, and the night air made her shiver.

He didn't bother to remove the robe. He just shoved it aside as he pressed her down against the bench. The cold stone bit into her back, and her hair spilled over the open sides, grazing the damp floor of the gazebo. She barely noticed the discomfort, although the edge of the bench stabbed into the small of her back, and her legs were unsupported.

Then he was there, between her legs, lifting them up around his waist as he bent over her, his hands on either side of her, his head ducked low, and his lips hot against her breasts. He sucked hungrily, not shielding his teeth, and though it hurt she wanted more. She pulled his head close, weaving her fingers through his black hair and around his ears, all the while pressing upward with her hips, seeking again the hardness her hands had discovered.

By the time she heard the grating of his zipper and the rustle of denim as he freed himself, she was spinning. Nothing existed but the point at which their bodies were to join. She locked her feet around his back and felt his muscles bunch beneath them. Something was tightening inside her, like a rope twisted to the breaking point, and tears streamed down her cheeks, mingling with perspiration in her tangled hair.

When he entered her, an unrestrained driving assault, the world turned white. Pain and pleasure rode in together on a bolt of lightning, and she shook with the force of it. She was barely aware of his few wild hard thrusts, too caught up in the shivering explosion that racked her own body, but almost immediately she heard him groan, and a new warmth flooded her. New spasms that somehow were part of her and yet not part of her pulsed inside her, and paradoxically, the intensity of the pleasure made her begin crying again.

Gradually the spinning white world grew calm and dark. Half standing, half bending, with the heels of his hands against the stone bench, he stayed above her. His head remained bowed, his eyes shut, his breathing labored. She didn't know what to say. She wanted *him* to say something. Anything.

Why didn't he kiss her? Why didn't he hold her? How could she feel so alone with him still inside her? It had happened too fast. She hadn't had time to control it, to understand it. Though it had been wonderful, it had also been violent and frightening, and she needed him to comfort her, to help her understand what had happened.

But he didn't. Finally she touched his damp hair with a tentative hand, and the gentle touch seemed to galvanize him. He reached back to unwind her legs and

pulled himself savagely away, letting her slippered feet
fall to the clammy floor. The cold air rushed in, harsh
where the heat of his body had been.

He turned away, his breath still ragged, and with a
growing sense of dismay she heard the low scratch of his
zipper, the dull click of his belt.

Ironically it was only now, when his back was to her,
when he refused to look at her, that her nakedness
seemed indecent. She fumbled with the ends of her robe
and swallowed a choking sob.

"Edan?" Her voice was thick with tears and fear.

He didn't turn around. Instead, he gripped the lattice of the gazebo and pressed his head against the
wood. His body was rigid, unyielding.

"Edan?"

"*What?*" He made the word a curse. He slammed
first his forehead, then his fist against the gazebo, and
the walls shuddered under the attack.

"What the hell do you want me to say, Nell? That I'm
sorry? Will that do any good? Then I'll say it. I'm a fool
and a bastard and I'm as sorry as bloody hell!"

Sorry? Oh, no... She had offered him everything she
had, body and soul, and he was *sorry?* She curled up on
the bench, her knees drawn up into her stomach, and
sobbed like the child he had said she was.

They were still like that, not two feet apart but frozen in miserable isolation, when her father found
them....

"WHAT ARE YOU DOING UP at this time of night?"

Light flooded the kitchen and she blinked, confused. The images in her mind had been so intense. It
was as if that night nine years ago was more real than
tonight could ever be. She blinked again and saw Edan

standing by the door, his hand on the light switch. He still wore his gray slacks and a thin black sweater, though he had shed his jacket. He clearly hadn't been to bed.

"It's three in the morning, Nell. What are you doing up?"

She sipped her milk and surreptitiously adjusted her nightshirt to cover a little more of her bare thighs.

"Well, it's only about midnight in California, remember. It'll take me a while to get used to Eastern standard time."

She took the mug to the sink. As she ran warm water to rinse out the last of the milk, she looked at him over her shoulder.

"How about you? Aren't you going to bed?"

"Soon." He perched on the edge of the kitchen table and watched her. Feeling his scrutiny, she wished she'd worn a robe. Her short nightshirt, just a pale blue T-shirt, was too revealing for comfort. Bending at the knee, she leaned over to grab the detergent.

"Where did you get those bruises?"

She whirled around, surprised. "What bruises?" She followed his eyes, which were focused on her upper thighs, and saw the faint purpling. "Oh, those."

"Yes. Those." He raised one brow. "Why? Do you have others?"

Smiling, she fingered the fading bruises. They had almost lost their tenderness. "Probably. Some of the kids I work with get kind of rough. And besides, I bruise easily. Some people do."

What a stupid remark! Heat suffused her cheeks as she remembered that he knew all too well how easily she bruised. After that night in the gazebo, her lower arms had been a mass of mottled marks where he had gripped her.

Of course, Edan had been bruised, too. Her father hadn't waited to ask any questions. He'd simply lashed out at Edan, knocking him to the gazebo floor. She had cried out, trying to explain that Edan hadn't hurt her, but her father hadn't listened. And Edan hadn't defended himself. He'd climbed slowly to his feet and stood there, anguished but mute. . . .

But he didn't seem to be remembering that now. "I heard you did counseling with troubled kids," he said. "Sounds like a tough job."

"Oh, no." She hastened to correct him. "It's wonderful. I love it. And they aren't bad kids, really. They're just so desperately unhappy. They can't believe anyone is ready to care about them."

"And you do?"

"Of course. They're only kids."

He glanced at the bruises. "Seems as if they aren't altogether grateful for your affection."

She dismissed the marks with a wave. "They're just testing, to see if I'll give up on them. They want to see if my love has strings. If it has limits."

He wore a quizzical expression. "And does it?"

She shook her head, thinking of the heartsick little boy who had given her these particular bruises. She had held him, murmuring words of acceptance, until he had stopped writhing and cursing and kicking. And then, finally feeling safe, he had begun to cry, releasing the pain he had held inside for so long.

"No," she said, a hint of sadness in her voice. "No limits. They can storm all they like. They have a right to be angry."

She looked away, embarrassed by the emotion that threatened to overcome her. She pulled a dishcloth off the drying rack and rubbed the mug. "It's awful, Edan. I was shocked at first. I hadn't realized people could be so cruel to kids."

He remained silent for a moment, and when he spoke his voice was mildly sarcastic. "I seem to remember when you thought your own childhood was the purest hell. Do you mean there are things tougher than being sent off to an exclusive boarding school? Tougher than being a Southern heiress from a broken home?"

She flushed and turned to face him. One brow was arched in his usual infuriating way, but she forced herself to remain calm. After all, he was right.

"I had a lot to learn," she said quietly.

In answer, he raised his eyebrow another millimeter.

"I like the job," she said, trying not to sound defensive. She *had* learned a lot. Let him believe her or not as he chose. "I like the kids." A warmth under her hands told her she had polished the mug enough.

"How much does it pay?"

She frowned. "That's none of your business."

"I think it is." He came to where she stood and put his hands over hers, stilling them. "That's as dry as it'll get, Nell. Tell me."

She gazed stupidly at the mug. "Tell you what?"

"Your dad expected me to look after you. Every month I mail you your fifty percent of the proceeds from Wildings Realty, and every month you make the checks over to the California Family Therapy Center. Why do you do that?"

She moved away. Her back toward him, she slid the mug into the cupboard. "I don't need it. The center does. It's as simple as that. Besides, I don't want it."

He made a small disgusted sound. "That's childish. It's your money. And you must need it. You can't make that much at your job."

She stared at him, raising her chin. Typical of him—running down whatever she was doing. The center couldn't afford to pay her much because it was struggling to pay its own bills. The psychiatrists there did much of their work free of charge, or at drastically reduced rates. They wanted to help people, not get rich. And so did she. If he couldn't understand that...

"I don't *want* it." She knew how immature she sounded, but she couldn't do any better. The subject was too sore; it probably always would be. Though her father had left her half of the company's proceeds, he had left full control of the business to Edan. Edan did all the work. She didn't want money she didn't earn, from a man who didn't care about her. Far better to donate it to a cause she believed in.

He clasped her shoulders with both hands. "Your father wanted you to have it. He wanted me to take care of you."

Tears pricked at her eyes, the overflow of a geyser of resentment.

"And you'd know what my father wanted a heck of a lot better than I would, wouldn't you, Edan? You were always his confidant, weren't you?" Her eyes narrowed. "You knew everything about him, even that his health was bad." She began to shake. She hoped he didn't think it was weakness. Far from it—it was fury. "Nobody bothered to tell *me* about my father's heart attacks. Nobody let me in on the little secret that he might die."

His grip tightened, and his brow contracted. "He didn't want to tell you. I explained that to you at the funeral. He didn't want you to know."

Murmuring an incoherent syllable of fury, she wrenched away and stalked to the door. There she turned, steeled her voice, willing it not to quiver, and gave him her coldest look.

"No, I'm sure he didn't. He didn't need me, did he? He had you. Well, that's fine. Because I don't need either of you. And I certainly don't need your damned money."

To her amazement he chuckled, a low throaty sound that reverberated through the big kitchen.

"Spoken like a true fifteen-year-old, Nellie-Belle. In fact, didn't you say something very similar back when you *were* fifteen? I think you vowed to find the Wilding treasure and show us all. Maybe your friendly ghost will turn up at the reunion and tell you where it is. Charlotte's planning a treasure hunt—did she mention that?"

Eleanor was surprised, though she hated to show it. Her grandmother had always pooh-poohed the legend of Captain Wilding's buried treasure and had hated the frequent hunts, which dug up her favorite bushes and mangled her smooth green lawn. Now she was planning a treasure hunt?

"No," she said caustically. "She didn't. As usual, *you* have all the information."

He grinned. "Well, I've had the advantage of proximity."

That did it. She flipped off the light, and his grin dissolved in the darkness.

"Fine," she retorted. "Then the ghost will probably do all his talking to you, too. In fact, with all this proximity, it's a wonder he hasn't already told you where the treasure is.''

It was so dark she didn't see him move. But when he spoke he was right next to her, his breath warm against her ear.

''What,'' he said, his voice rippling with amusement, ''makes you think he hasn't?''

CHAPTER THREE

"WELCOME TO WILDINGS."

It was only eight o'clock, and Eleanor was halfway down the stairs when she heard Edan greet the first arrivals of the morning. Squeezing the newel post at the landing, she took a deep breath. She should have known he'd beat her to the door, eager to play host.

"Edan!" The other voice was gay and melodic, conveying a world of delight. "Honestly, it's just too mean of you, getting better looking every time I turn around! You'd already broken all our poor little hearts before you were twenty, you old devil."

In spite of herself, Eleanor grinned, and her annoyance lifted. She knew that voice.

"Gina!" She hurried down the last few steps, a welcoming smile on her lips.

"Eleanor?" The woman who had stepped inside frowned prettily. "Why, Eleanor Wilding, is that really you?"

Nodding, Eleanor gave Gina a big hug, surprised at how happy she was to see her cousin. Back when they were kids she'd been terribly jealous of Gina's dark good looks and breezy charm, and she had always been quick to read insult into Gina's lazy comments. The thought flickered through her mind now that she must have been a very difficult teenager indeed. She found herself hoping that Gina didn't hold that against her.

Most likely she didn't. Gina had always been too indolent to be intolerant, and clearly she hadn't changed a bit. She was as gorgeous as ever, with her dark cloud of hair resting on the shoulders of her bright red jumpsuit. She pulled back, giving Eleanor a once-over.

"Why, you look wonderful," Gina said, smiling generously. "You've really burst into full bloom, haven't you, honey? Isn't she just a picture, Edan?"

He appeared to consider. "Picture of what?" But his eyes were uptilted at the corners, teasing.

Gina clicked her tongue and thrust her suitcases at Edan. "Hush now, you annoying man. Don't mind him, Eleanor. He noticed, all right. Men always do, especially men like him. Take that upstairs, Edan, while I talk to Eleanor."

"Yes'm," he said meekly, sweeping a mock bow. "But don't you ladies forget to answer the door. Charlotte's not ready to come down yet, and the thundering horde is due here any minute."

"I think we can manage," Eleanor said, clipping the words. As if she couldn't be trusted to answer the doorbell!

Gina eyed her narrowly when they went into the parlor and sat on the love seat. "Hmm. Still allergic, I see," she said. "That's too bad."

"Allergic?"

"To our resident hunk." Gina tossed her curls back and smiled. "I'd thought maybe it was one of those childhood allergies you'd grow out of."

Eleanor flushed. It was true. Every time she was around Edan she acted like an adolescent. She was going to have to work on that.

"Sorry. It's probably just a terminal case of sibling rivalry." Frank Hubert, the psychiatrist who was her boss back at the center, should hear her now. He'd applaud the courage that allowed her to say that.

Frank had known, better than Eleanor herself, that she needed to come home again, needed to straighten all this out before she could ever make a good counselor. But had Frank realized, she wondered, how hard it would be to face Edan again? Some ghosts wouldn't rest simply because you asked them to.

"Well, honey, you two aren't really siblings, you know. No blood relation at all. With a dreamboat like Edan, I would think you'd want to keep that in mind." Gina smoothed a pant leg over a trim thigh and sighed. "I certainly thanked my lucky stars often enough that I wasn't his cousin."

"I remember." Eleanor's smile felt slightly forced. She definitely remembered. Gina's blatant interest in Edan had been like fuel poured over the fire of Eleanor's antagonism. It had been maddening. Every darn girl who met Edan fell for him.

She bit her lower lip, suddenly hearing herself objectively. Back at the center, Frank wouldn't have let that revealing statement go unchallenged. Time for a reality check, Eleanor, he'd say in his gently teasing baritone. *Had* every girl been after Edan, or had little Nell's own pining desire simply made it seem that way?

"Not that it did me a bit of good." Gina sighed again, a deep inhale and exhale that strained against her tight suit. "He kept his home life and his love life strictly separate, as best I could tell. Made sense at the time, I suppose, but now that we're all grown up..." She let the sentence dangle, a wicked gleam sparkling in her brown eyes.

Eleanor turned away from that gleam and stared out the window at the sun-dappled front yard. So Gina hadn't even guessed. Edan and Eleanor's father had kept the secret well, the secret that they had decided was too dirty, too terrible to tell.

They were going to pretend the night at the gazebo had never happened, her father had told her. She was never to mention it to anyone. She had stared at him, disbelieving. Pretend it had never happened? How could she? How could Edan?

The horrible charade was almost more than she could stand. She couldn't eat. She couldn't sleep. It had been the most important night of her life, and they were going to erase it, to freeze it out of existence with their glacial silences.

Only one thing lay beyond their control: her body. Suppose her body already held the proof that the night *had* been real? She remembered her father's last tight-lipped question: "Did you bother to protect her?" Edan had shaken his head stiffly, as though it were made of painful steel rather than flesh and blood.

A baby. Although the thought had terrified her, for two crazy weeks she had almost hoped it was true. At least then they would be forced to acknowledge what had happened. For two weeks their parents had watched her, staring at her as if she had grown horns. For those same two weeks Edan had refused to look at her, his gray eyes as bleak as a winter sky smothered in unshed snow. When he'd had to look at her, he looked through her.

And then, when her insane hopes were dashed and there was nothing left to wait for, they had bundled her off, for the first time, to boarding school.

Banished. Disgraced. It was horrible. No one wanted her, it seemed. Away from Gran, who'd been the only consistent port in the storm of her life. Away from Wildings, except for vacations. Away from Edan.

It was particularly galling that Edan had remained at Wildings, apparently absolved and reinstated. Eleanor clearly had been identified as the "problem" and wasn't to be forgiven. And so she had vowed she would never forgive *them*.

"Whoops. We promised Edan we'd get that!" Gina hopped to her feet and plucked at Eleanor's sleeve. "Come on, hostess, greet your guests."

Abruptly the present came back into focus as the doorbell pealed again. Though Eleanor had no first cousins, her family tree was thick with third and fourth cousins, cousins by marriage, and some with such convoluted relationships that they were essentially cousins by choice. Wilding reunions were always noisy and crowded.

With effort Eleanor stood up, arranging her mouth in a suitable smile. The doorbell rang a third impatient time as she reached the hall, and she made a quick grab for the knob just as another darker hand did the same.

Edan's palm closed over her knuckles, pressing her flesh into the cold metal of the doorknob. A queer tingling numbness shot up her arm. He stood so close that she could smell the faint smoky aroma that clung to his sweater. He must have been laying the fire in the living-room hearth.

She inhaled deeply, drinking in the scent, before she could stop herself. Oh, Lord, she should never have come! Four days of this—this stupid weakness, this agonizing awareness, this eternal war of anger and desire. She'd never make it.

She wriggled her hand, trying to release the doorknob and let him open it. But his hold tightened.

"How about a joint effort, Nellie?" His voice was unnaturally warm, and she looked up at him warily.

His gray eyes were warm, too, and he wore a half smile that was surprisingly devoid of sarcasm. Suddenly she knew he wasn't just talking about the door.

"We can do it. It's simple, really." A laugh hid in the undercurrents of his voice, but it was, for once, a friendly sound, and the fist of confusion loosened its grip on her heart. "Just teamwork and timing, that's all. Just don't pull when I push, zig when I zag, or yin when I yang. Here's the plan. Twist twenty degrees to the right on the count of three. Ready? One...two..."

It was ridiculous. Against her better judgment she smiled, surrendered to the impulse to chuckle and added her voice to his.

"Three," they said in unison and opened the door to a crowd of Wildings. And perhaps, she thought, to a temporary truce.

IT WAS THE NINTH INNING, and her team was losing ten to seven when she came to bat. Edan, who was pitching, winked broadly at her.

"Better bring the outfield in," he called, loud enough for her to hear, but hardly loud enough to be audible out in the field. "Pitchers, you know. Terrible batters."

"You should know," she called back airily, and tapped her bat on the plate with as much savoir faire as she could muster. It didn't help that she was one lousy batter. She'd been up five times today, with only a single to show for it.

Her poor performance hadn't spoiled the afternoon, though. Wilding family reunions always began with the softball game, and she had to admit it was the perfect icebreaker. It was hard to feel stilted when everybody's shirt was covered in dirt. And it was impossible to be unsociable with a guy when you had just slid through his legs into third. By the seventh-inning stretch, they were all relaxed and happy.

The weather cooperated, too. Springs here were crisp, the wind light enough to blow hair soothingly away from sweaty brows, and the sun gentle enough to pinken noses becomingly without burning.

This late in the game it was getting cooler, though, and the moss swayed harder from the sweeping branches of the live oaks. A gust of wisteria-scented air swept over home plate just as Edan's first pitch sailed neatly past Eleanor's midriff.

"Strike one!"

She bit her lip and crouched lower, concentrating. He had been practicing.

She caught a piece of the next one and tapped it into the no-man's-land between the bases and the outfield. Her legs raced and her ponytail flew behind her as she dashed for first base. She made it with only a heartbeat to spare and, panting but pleased, she winked at Edan.

Chuckling, he faced the plate, ready to take on the next batter. She puffed lightly, hands on her thighs, trying to ease her aching lungs.

"You sure fill out your baseball duds better than you did the last time I saw you, Eleanor." A hand cupped the curve of her hip insinuatingly.

She whirled around, evading the presumptuous touch. Allen Ridgeway, first baseman and third cousin. Or was it fourth? Second twice-removed? She'd always loathed him too much to bother figuring it out.

"That shouldn't be surprising," she said, her eyes passing over Allen to return to Edan, who was about to pitch. "I was probably only ten the last time you saw me."

"Yeah." Allen laughed. "Prickly as a thorn, you were, and shaped like one, too. Glad to see you've softened up." His hand crept back to her hip.

She batted the hand away without even turning around. "Looks can be deceiving, Allen. Full-grown roses have thorns like bayonets. Bet your wife knows that." She cast a meaningful glance toward the lawn chairs, where Allen's pretty wife, Monica, sat sulking. Monica had been one of the few guests who had refused to play. It didn't take a detective to see that the Ridgeway marriage was rocky.

And likely to be rockier, if he had to explain to Monica why Eleanor Wilding had slammed her elbow into his ribs. But apparently Allen wasn't that dense. He subsided, contenting himself with hollering catcalls to distract the batter.

His tactics didn't work. Miraculously the batter hit a long one, and it rolled away from the fielders, skipping down toward the river. Adrenaline shot through Eleanor as she realized what had happened. The bases were loaded—she could be the tying run. Around the infield she flew, and out of the corner of her eye she could see Edan, like the still center of a whirlpool, laughing and calling, urging his fielders to hurry.

The catcher was hopelessly out of position when Eleanor rounded third, and she saw him throw the ball to Edan, who was the only one close enough to tag her. So, she thought, after all these innings it had come down to just the two of them....

Home plate seemed to stretch away from her, as if it were on the thin end of a rubber band about to break.

Her thighs burned; her lungs throbbed. Edan was so close ... so close.

She and Edan collided at home plate, in a hopeless tangle of arms and legs and dirt. She had no idea whether she had scored. She was underneath him, her legs stretched out toward the plate, but he sprawled over her, pinning her torso under his chest, and his body blocked her view.

Everyone was yelling at once—"She's safe!" "She's out!" "Are you blind? She's safe!" She tried to care. If, beyond Edan's body, her toe had touched home plate, she had tied the game. It mattered. It did....

But it *didn't* matter, not to her. As her eyes met his, the voices around them evaporated, like mist under a too-bright sun. Her senses registered only Edan, the way his gray eyes were almost black, the way her body fit perfectly between his strong thighs. The way the heavy odor of wisteria braided with the masculine sweat of him, and the way his heart drummed against her breast.

His body lay heavily on her, and though it paralyzed her, it was a weight she remembered, a weight that felt more wonderful than freedom, more necessary than air.

"She's safe! Let her up, Edan. It's a tie game. She got the edge of the base with her foot. She's safe."

The voices finally broke through and, blinking, Edan eased his body up, untangling his legs from hers. She didn't know how he managed it; her own body no longer seemed under her control.

He held out a hand and, because there was nothing else to do, she took it.

"Congratulations," he said, his breathing ragged. "You're safe."

Safe? She let him pull her to her feet. How ironic. She'd never in her life felt less so.

As THE SUN SET over the Mississippi, layering the sky with strips of peach and purple, the whole Wilding clan sat at picnic tables or on blankets and ate fried chicken from wicker baskets.

Eleanor had chosen a blanket as far away from Edan's as possible. He didn't seem to miss her. Gina kept him company, her red jumpsuit the only bright spot in the grimy gray T-shirts of the softball players. As lazy as ever, Gina had napped during the game, emerging for dinner refreshed and cool and ready for serious flirtation. Occasionally Eleanor heard Edan's low laugh over the general banter, and whenever she did she laughed more herself, as though to drown out the sound.

No laughter came from the Ridgeway blanket, she noticed. Allen and Monica ate in stony silence, and for a depressing moment Eleanor wondered whether she ought to join them and try to act as buffer between husband and wife. But she assumed that Monica Ridgeway knew about Allen's indiscriminate flirtations, and she decided it would just make things worse.

What about their daughter? They had arrived this morning with a surly adolescent, whose unbecoming clothes, spiked hair and pouting mouth proclaimed her dissatisfaction to the whole world. A twinge of sympathy had pinched Eleanor at her first sight of Kelly Ridgeway. She knew that look, that I-don't-care-what-you-think look. That defiance that meant only one thing—you can't reject me, because I rejected you first.

Why wasn't Kelly sitting with her parents? Eleanor scanned the blankets, but the girl wasn't among the picknicking crowd. Where was she?

It was dusk and getting harder to see, but finally Eleanor spotted her, a dark isolated figure at the edge of the bluff overlooking the river. Excusing herself from the cousins sharing her blanket, Eleanor strolled over and sat beside Kelly.

"Nice, isn't it?"

Kelly looked up without smiling. "It's okay." She returned to her scrutiny of the river.

Eleanor studied the girl covertly. She must be about thirteen. A tough age—ninety percent of the time desperate to be treated like an adult, and the other ten percent scared as hell to leave childhood behind. All kids went through it.

But Kelly's attitude hinted at something more. Eleanor watched the way Kelly ripped up blades of grass with tense fingers. Her work at the center was usually with younger kids, but every instinct told Eleanor that beneath Kelly's faddish black clothes and bright red lipstick was a very unhappy little girl.

"Have you been to Wildings before?"

This time Kelly didn't bother to look up. "Yeah. Three times. Three of these dorky reunions. Before that we lived in Arizona, thank heavens."

Eleanor stifled a smile. She hadn't been too fond of the reunions herself at Kelly's age. She hadn't been much older than Kelly when Edan had appeared, Edan the consummate athlete, the perfect student, the gracious young master, showing off and showing her up. And her father, always standing beside him, his arm around Edan's broad young shoulders, so unabashedly proud.

"Yeah," Eleanor responded, picking up the rhythm of Kelly's speech. Kelly wouldn't get any lectures on The Importance of Family from her. Lectures simply alienated kids, forced them into ever more defiant postures.

"Family reunions aren't exactly a thrill a minute, are they?"

They sat silently for a minute. Eleanor skipped a small rock down the bluff.

"I didn't think we'd have to come this year," Kelly said suddenly. "I was sure my folks would be divorced by now. I don't know what they're waiting for."

Though her heart sank and her arms twitched from an instinctive urge to reach out to the younger girl, Eleanor forced herself to show no reaction. This was just like the kids back at the center, trying to shock her with her tough cynicism. She put a blade of grass between her teeth, buying a little time as she tried to filter any hint of pity out of her voice. Pity would only infuriate Kelly.

"Really?" Eleanor managed to sound only mildly interested. "Your parents are going to get a divorce?"

"They certainly ought to!" Apparently Eleanor's tone had reassured Kelly, for she let a more natural note of anger creep into her voice. "They can't stand each other. All they do is fight and yell and take it all out on me. I'm sick of it."

"I'll bet." Eleanor's heart twisted. Kelly had, in her simple way, summed the situation up very well. The same old story, repeating itself over and over in miserable households everywhere, every day. How could you tell the scared suffering kids that it wasn't their fault? Could anyone have convinced *her*, back when it had been her parents fighting and yelling and taking it all out on her? Probably not. "Sounds terrible."

"It is," Kelly agreed with black emphasis. "It's a major bummer."

"Kelly Anne Ridgeway!" A strident voice broke into their conversation, and they swiveled to see Monica

Ridgeway standing, arms akimbo, beside the picnic basket. "Didn't I tell you to clean this up? Why can't I ever ask you to do something and have you *do* it?"

Kelly turned away from the voice and sighed. "See what I mean?" she mumbled mutinously. "She's not really mad at me. She's mad at Dad. But he just walks away from her, so she's got all this yelling left over, and I get it."

Eleanor was surprised to see a small wry grin on the girl's bright red lips. "Wow. Lucky you," she said, low enough that Monica couldn't hear.

"Yeah. Lucky me." Kelly stood up, wiping dirt and grass from the back of her thighs. "See ya."

Eleanor watched as Kelly sauntered over to her mother. Monica's whining voice carried on the light wind, enough for Eleanor to hear the tenor but not the content of her complaints. Kelly didn't respond. She just bent down and repacked the basket with exaggerated care. Eleanor bit back a smile. That kid had spunk. Maybe she'd be a survivor.

Kelly certainly understood more about her parents than Eleanor had at that age. Eleanor didn't even like to remember the years before her parents had divorced. In some ways, those years had been even harder than the years after their remarriages. Her mother had been much happier in her new marriage, with her new family, and certainly her father had been happier, too, when he'd married Edan's mother.

And if all those happy new families had left no room for little Eleanor, well, who cared? At first, she had been shunted between her stepfather's home in Louisiana, and Wildings, where her father had continued to live. Then, after the episode with Edan, boarding school had become her home. Her only peaceful times had come during vacations, when they had let her stay at Wildings.

Wildings. She breathed deeply, filling her lungs with the cool spring evening air. How many nights had she sat here on the bluff watching the sun go down over the Mississippi? She'd seen sunsets of angry red, of melancholy violet, of festive orange, and even a few—a very few—that were a peaceful dove gray. Thank heaven her self-imposed exile had ended.

For the first time, she wondered whether she might be able to find a job here in Mississippi. She'd miss the center, but there must be other centers that would welcome her help. Frank, she knew, would understand. He'd even hinted at the possibility that, once home, she might find it difficult to leave again. She had rejected the notion vehemently then, but already she could feel Wildings wrapping itself around her, clinging, claiming—

"Chilly?"

She felt Edan's hands on her shoulders before she saw him.

"No," she said, tilting her head back. He loomed above her, a tall dark shadow against the moonlit sky. "Not really."

Ignoring her answer, he rubbed her upper arms briskly, sending shivers across her back and chest. Funny, she really hadn't noticed how cold, or how dark, it had become. She heard the rustle of suede, and then he dropped his jacket across her shoulders and sat down at her side.

"Thanks." She burrowed into the jacket. It was still warm from his body, and it smelled wonderfully male, like leather and shaving cream.

"I saw you talking to Kelly," he said. "Was it a personal talk or a professional one?"

She flicked him a glance. He didn't miss much, did he? "Personal," she said. "But she does need somebody to talk to, doesn't she?"

He leaned on one elbow, resting his other arm on his knee. "Does she? I thought maybe she just needed a swift kick in the rear."

"Edan!" She was incredulous. "What a mean thing to say! Kelly's parents are probably on the verge of divorce."

"Yeah. And?"

She frowned. "And she's all mixed up, damn it. Can't you see that?" His lazy indifference irritated her. "Oh, never mind. I must have forgotten—you never did have any sympathy for the underdog, did you?"

He chuckled and adjusted his weight, resting his cheek on his knuckles. "Maybe I'm just not sure who's the underdog here."

She peered at him in the darkness. He seemed to be smiling. "What does that mean?"

"It means I think Kelly Ridgeway is a very bright, very strong kid. I think she's about twice as tough as either of her parents and about ten times as sensible." He shifted again, and his profile caught the moonlight. "It means I think that in the long run Kelly will be fine, although I'm not laying any odds on Monica, who strikes me as a professional martyr, or on Allen, who seems to be having a particularly obnoxious mid-life crisis."

Eleanor relaxed. He was so right that she couldn't help laughing. "Maybe you should be the psychologist. That's pretty good for a layman."

"I keep my eyes open," he said. "And when I saw him pawing you at first base this afternoon, it sure looked like mid-life dementia to me."

She clicked her tongue. "Well, thanks," she said, trying to sound offended. "A man has to be suffering from dementia to want to paw me?"

He nudged her with his foot. "You know what I mean."

"As a matter of fact, I do," she admitted. "And I think you're right about Kelly. I was just sitting here thinking how perceptive she is about her parents' problems. She even recognizes that sometimes when they seem to be mad at her they're really mad at each other." Against her will, a wistful note crept into her voice. "I never knew that, never understood that, at her age."

"No," he said quietly. "Neither did I."

She opened her mouth, instinctively protesting, but somehow she managed to stop the stupid words from tumbling out. Neither did he? The insight stunned her. Never, ever, in all these years, had she thought of Edan as having been a troubled youngster. She knew that his parents had divorced, obviously, but he had always seemed so strong, so confident. Was it possible he had lived through the same destructive scenes that had marred her own childhood?

But even as she sat openmouthed, registering the shock, another part of her accepted it easily. Of course it was possible. It was almost inevitable. The only real surprise here was that she hadn't thought of it before.

Frank would tell her it was natural, that it was easy to be objective and analytical about a patient's life, but much harder to bring that objectivity to your own. And yet... And yet somehow she was embarrassed, ashamed that she had been so wrapped up in her own misery that she had given no thought to his.

"Edan," she began, reaching out a hand to him. In the darkness she misjudged the distance, and instead of touching his arm she met the inner edge of his thigh, high, near the crease where his leg met his hip. His muscles tightened under her fingers, and before she could pull away, he dropped his hand over hers, pressing it into the warm rough denim.

"What, Nellie?" His voice was low.

But she was too confused to answer. What had she wanted to say? Her thoughts were garbled. If she had tried to speak she would have uttered gibberish.

Under her palm his leg was warm. She could hardly remember what they had been talking about. She knew only one thing, with sudden desperate clarity. She wanted him. She wanted to lie with him, here on the bluff in the moonlight, and make love. Could she say that?

Of course not. But she couldn't say anything else, either. What had that nonsense been about Kelly Ridgeway's parents? Kelly's parents didn't matter; even her own confused childhood didn't matter. Nothing mattered except that she wanted him so much it hurt.

Had it begun this afternoon, when their bodies had collided on the playing field? His weight on hers had started a dull ache that seemed only to grow with every hour. Now his firm muscles were under her hand, and an almost imperceptible quiver ran through his leg. This afternoon, those thighs had pinned her down...

But it hadn't started this afternoon. It had started years and years ago.

Ten years. From the day they met. Those ten years of thwarted longing had created a silver dagger of desire, and, now that the barrier of anger was down, it stabbed her with a piercing need.

"What?" he said again, his voice urgent, the muscles in his thigh clenching tighter. "Tell me."

She shook her head, still breathing through her mouth, trying to ride out the fierce spasms of desire. This was insane. This was worse than insane. What was happening to her? Where were the defenses she had built to protect herself? This one small insight into Edan's life didn't change anything. So he had been lonely, too. So what? That didn't mean that she . . . that they . . .

She climbed clumsily to her feet. "Go in," she managed. "We have to go in." His jacket fell to the ground with a rustling whisper.

She got as far as the gazebo. But there, under the ripened wisteria, he caught her. He pulled her off balance, and she stumbled heavily against him.

"No, we don't," he murmured. "We're not through yet."

And then his mouth found hers.

CHAPTER FOUR

As HIS HEAD BENT toward her, the moment had the surreal quality of a dream. Time seemed to speed and yet to drag. Her heart raced, but her body was locked in a torpor she couldn't control. And, like a dreamer who tossed and moaned but couldn't awaken, she was incapable of resistance.

She registered every detail, but numbly. The way moonlight wrapped him in a watery glow. The way the gazebo settled itself around them with a low creaking, and the whisper as a garland of moss slipped from its branch.

Her lungs were filled with the complicated aroma of leather and flowers, and she feared she could not subsist, even in a dream, on such thickened air.

But she wasn't dreaming. Paradoxically, the kiss that had first lulled her into a helpless languor soon forced her into a painful awareness. This was not the Edan of her dreams, no shadowy phantom of lost innocence that melted away with the morning. This was a man. Locked in his embrace, *she* was the one who was melting.

She clung to him weakly. He was so tall, his shoulders so taut under her hands. She had almost forgotten.

His lips were hard, his breath hot as he kissed her, and he took her with a fevered violence. Back and forth his mouth swept over hers, trailing the faint burn of evening stubble across her soft cheeks like a brand.

He parted her lips, probing with fiery mastery until he owned the very breath she dared to breathe. He traced the tingling ridge of her teeth; he claimed the sensitive inner rim of her mouth. He sucked the tip of her tongue and pulled hungrily at the throbbing fullness of her lower lip.

Though his attentions never strayed from her mouth, her body began to quiver.

"Edan." Moaning softly into his mouth, she pressed closer to him. Her blood pounded relentlessly toward her midsection, and she was filled with need.

His lips lifted, just enough for the cold air to tease at the wetness he left behind. Bereft, she opened her eyes slowly.

"Edan?"

In answer, he moved back. His eyes were very dark, like the black smoke from an oil fire, giving her no clue as to what he was feeling.

What did he see in her eyes? Surely they smoldered with something more blatant. Perhaps not, since his gaze revealed no sign of recognition. Gradually, as he remained silent, she felt her senses settling, her blood receding. Blinking to focus her vision, she ran her tongue across swollen lips that felt maddeningly incapable of words.

Still he stared at her, and a spark of embarrassment, or possibly anger, flashed out of the embers of passion.

She dropped her hands to her hips. "Well?"

Moonlight caught on his small one-sided smile, and the glint was cold. "Well, what?"

She backed up. "What was that all about?"

His smile broadened but grew no warmer. "Nothing."

"Nothing?" Her hands tightened into fists. "You call that nothing?"

He leaned against the gazebo, the old wood creaking under his weight. "It was just a kiss, Nellie-Belle. I suppose it's not nothing, but I fail to see why you're so indignant. It's hardly a hanging offense."

She shook her head, bewildered by his abrupt change. Only minutes ago, his kiss had been like... She swallowed. Like what?

"I know. It's just that..." She trailed off, suddenly feeling foolish. She opened her fists and let her hands fall to her sides. No need to stand there looking like some wrathful fishwife. It *had* been just a kiss.

She put her hands behind her back and threaded her fingers through the lattice of the gazebo. "Why did you do it?"

"Kiss you?" He tilted his head and looked out at the river, presenting his strong profile to her. "I don't know. Maybe the romance of the Mississippi in the moonlight?" He turned back and ran his eyes slowly down her clay-stained jersey. "Or maybe just your unparalleled charms?"

Now she glanced away. That wasn't funny. She knew how she looked: much more the tomboy he had always despised than an irresistible siren.

His voice deepened. "Or maybe it's because I *didn't* kiss you all those years ago. Maybe because, as I said, this time it's not a hanging offense."

She frowned. "*This* time?"

His eyes glittered. "Well, if someone—like your father, for instance—had wanted to get technical about it, it *was* a hanging offense back then, you know."

She almost choked. She squeezed the lattice until it bit into her fingers. "That's ridiculous!"

"Is it?" His words were as rough as the unsanded wood under her hands. "Don't tell me you hadn't thought of it. I'm sure that was half the fun of it for you. Maybe more than half, at least subconsciously."

Her cheeks flamed as she took in his meaning.

"Of all the stupid things you've ever said, Edan Bond, that is the stupidest. Do you really think that I—"

"Yes. I really do."

"Then you vastly overrate your importance." She was furious and strangely wounded by his words. Could he actually believe that? "And you underrate my intelligence. I may have been a kid, but I knew full well my father was besotted with you and that nothing could come between you. Look how quickly he forgave you! Overnight!"

"Hardly overnight," he corrected blandly.

"Forty-eight hours, then? Of course, if you'd murdered me, I suppose it might have taken longer—maybe a week...." To her dismay her voice broke. "But," she said through angry tears, "he would have forgiven you anything."

His eyes no longer glittered. They were narrowed to fierce slits that even the moonlight couldn't reach. "You hated that, didn't you? Well, this might make you feel better. Maybe he forgave me—"

"Maybe?" She laughed, a brittle unnatural sound. "Maybe? He left you in control of everything, didn't he?"

"Shut up." He grabbed her upper arms, and his voice was as tight as his grip. "Listen to me. You probably won't understand this, but I want you to hear it, just this once. You're right. Your father tried to forgive me. He was a good man. But I never—do you hear me?—never forgave myself."

She opened her mouth, ready to toss hot words back at him, but there were none to be found. She simply stared, her chest heaving impotently.

"And I never will." With a low disgusted sound, he let go of her and began to walk away into the darkness.

He was only a pale image when she was finally able to speak.

"As long as you're being honest," she called, "let's hear the rest of it. You never forgave yourself." Her attempt at proud defiance was failing miserably as the words came out thin and quavery. "But you never forgave me, either."

He stopped.

"No," he said, his voice carrying with merciless precision over the gathering mist. "Not you, either."

CHARLOTTE WAS HOLDING court in the front parlor, surrounded by her family. Eleanor tried to slip in unnoticed, but Charlotte saw her, of course, and summoned her to a chair at her side. A frown puckering between her blue eyes, the old woman scanned Eleanor's flushed face and then darted a look toward Edan.

Eleanor followed her gaze. Edan must have arrived just ahead of her, and yet he already looked completely at ease, as if he never lost his temper, and certainly not in the past five minutes. He straddled the seat of a straight-backed chair, murmuring something to Gina, who grinned at him, positively purring. With a cry of delight, little Nicholas Wilding, a distant cousin, clambered onto Edan's back and locked his hands around

Edan's neck. Undisturbed, Edan reached up lazily to tweak the boy's ear and went on talking.

The lord of the manor. All he needed was a couple of loyal bloodhounds dozing at his feet and an aged retainer to shuffle in with his brandy. No, forget the aged retainer. Monica Ridgeway appeared at his shoulder, proffering a tumbler of amber liquid. Eleanor turned away. When Edan next went looking for a moonlight kiss, how would he ever decide between his two eager handmaidens?

She met her grandmother's eyes, which held a question. Suspecting that Charlotte could probably read her thoughts, she wrinkled her nose sheepishly.

"Some kind of magnetic field, do you think?"

Charlotte smiled. "His path's littered with them. They quite fling themselves at his feet."

Eleanor raised her brows. "He'll have to be careful not to trip, then, won't he?"

Charlotte chuckled, took Eleanor's hand and patted it. "Now then, children," she called, encompassing everyone from three to sixty. "We're all here, so let's begin."

She had raised her voice only a couple of notches, but the murmur in the room died down instantly. Even Gina turned, wresting her attention from Edan. Charlotte Wilding had officially hosted the family reunions for as long as Eleanor could remember, and her authority was absolute.

Eleanor relaxed slightly, soothed by the sense of unalterable continuity and lulled by the dear familiar Southern accent. No one in her generation had much of an accent anymore, and that was really too bad. It was a soft slow sound, infinitely ladylike and yet full of velvet strength.

"So I've decided we'll have a treasure hunt this year," Charlotte said, and Eleanor realized she hadn't been listening.

A low whisper of excitement rippled through the room. Wildings treasure hunts were always popular, though only the very young children believed there actually was a treasure. Little Nicholas, still on Edan's shoulders, bucked and whooped.

"Let's try to put our minds to it, shall we? It would please me to find Captain Wilding's treasure this year," Charlotte said, squeezing Eleanor's hand. "I'm not well, and I can't be sure how many more reunions I'll see."

This time the murmur was louder, and full of dismay. Eleanor didn't speak. She clutched her grandmother's hand and stared at Charlotte, afraid to give her fears voice.

Others found words more easily. "What are you talking about, Charlotte Wilding?" one of the older cousins said with asperity. "You'll be here forever, and you know it."

Charlotte shook her head, meeting Eleanor's eyes. "No, I won't, Marlene," she said, but she was clearly speaking to Eleanor. "I've had two strokes already, and the doctors aren't promising anything."

Strokes. Eleanor felt as if her heart was refusing to beat. "No..." she whispered, pleading with her stinging eyes and her clammy hands as much as with her voice. "No, Gran."

"Yes, honey," Charlotte said softly. She rubbed Eleanor's cold hand. "But it's all right."

The room was full of movement, full of sound, as the family reacted to the news. Numbly Eleanor watched the faces around her—wide eyes, crumpled brows, mouths shaped in small circles of surprise. All registered horror, sadness, shock.

All except one.

She met his gaze across the tumult. His gray eyes were serious, somber, but not surprised. She pressed her lips together. Of course. Edan had known already. He always knew. And now he was looking at her with—what was it?—pity. Pity that, once again, little Nell was the last to know. Briefly a surge of anger overpowered her misery, and she clenched her teeth so tightly her jaws hurt.

"Eleanor, look at me."

Charlotte's crisp words were obviously a command, and Eleanor obeyed unthinkingly. To her dismay, a haze of tears warped her vision, and she blinked rapidly, trying to hide them.

"Why didn't you tell me, Gran? I would have come sooner. I would have come right away."

Her grandmother's smile was wry, her own blue eyes sparkling suspiciously. "I knew it would be hard for you."

"You told Edan." The minute the sentence was out of her mouth, Eleanor flushed. She hadn't meant to sound petulant.

"I didn't *tell* him," Charlotte said. "He was here when it happened."

Eleanor's flush deepened. Although Charlotte's voice had held no rebuke, Eleanor's own conscience forced her to face the truth. Edan had been here; she had not. It was as simple as that.

And thank heavens he had. If her grandmother had been here alone, unable to call for help... The image burned into her mind; she squeezed her eyes shut, hoping to escape it.

Her hand trembled, and Charlotte gripped it harder, as though she could transfer strength, finger to finger.

"Steady, honey," Charlotte said. "You're here now."

Eleanor met her grandmother's smile with a watery grateful one of her own. Yes, she was here now. She had come home—this time before it was too late—and she wasn't going to run away again. She gazed at Edan, who was comforting a weeping Gina, and swallowed her own tears. No more running—no matter how many old ghosts came out to haunt her.

"THIS CAPTAIN GUY must have been a real dork."

Kelly Ridgeway listlessly poked at the azalea bushes with a long twig. Eleanor, who was scouting around inside the old slave cabin, looked out the window. "Think so?"

Kelly sighed heavily and poked again, shaking her twig fiercely until she knocked several blossoms onto the ground.

"Absolutely. Major dork. If he was so crazy about this Celia person, why didn't he just marry her?" She stabbed a fallen blossom repeatedly, until its peach petals were bruised and dirty. "You sure you got your legend right? Maybe he already knew what a joke the whole 'wedded bliss' thing is. Maybe joining the army sounded like more fun."

Eleanor stuck her head out of the cabin door. Her sympathy aroused by Kelly's obvious lack of friends, she had volunteered to be the girl's partner for the morning's treasure hunt, and she was trying hard not to regret the decision. Kelly clearly found the "ghost thing" a big bore and had spent the past hour grumbling.

"Maybe," Eleanor said equably, plopping down on the top step and brushing her dusty palms on her shorts. "But I think the legend's more romantic the way it is."

She leaned her head back, enjoying the fresh air and sunlight after the musty dimness of the cabin. Blowing a stray hair out of her eyes, she wiped a bead of perspiration from her upper lip.

Dirty work. And it had probably been a waste of time; the ghost hadn't ever, not in a hundred years, been sighted here. He was always reported at the gazebo. But everybody else was scouring the ground around the gazebo. Edan and Gina were even prying up the floorboards.

"Well, why didn't he marry her? She was pregnant, wasn't she? I mean, that's the legend, isn't it?"

Kelly sat on the step below Eleanor, digging shallow gullies in the dirt with the end of her stick. Eleanor smiled, recognizing a keener interest than Kelly had intended to betray.

"I think that part is more than legend," she said. "Celia Galsworthy, who was visiting here at Wildings, definitely died of a miscarriage. She was all alone down at the gazebo in the middle of the night. No one even knew she was pregnant."

"Not even Captain Mr. Wonderful Wilding?"

Eleanor shrugged. "He never got a chance to say. He was killed at Gettysburg. He and Celia fell in love before he went off to war, and he'd written her father for permission to marry her. But she was engaged to someone else back in Charleston, where her family lived, and her father's letter refusing the Captain's request arrived a few days after Celia died."

"Bummer." But Kelly's tone wasn't all that sarcastic, and her eyes were sad.

"Yeah." Eleanor looked across the wide expanse of green lawn, bejeweled with ruby azaleas and amethyst wisteria. In the distance the gazebo was shaded by the graceful branches of an ancient oak. Beauty and sadness had coexisted here for many generations.

She thought of her tiny, fragile grandmother, resting upstairs while the rest of the family frolicked on this foolish treasure hunt. Eleanor had wanted to stay with her, but Charlotte had insisted that she join the search. As if she cared about all that now! Unless Captain Wilding had buried a chest full of miracles, full of health and happiness and hope, his treasure was worthless.

She pulled her attention back to Kelly, who was waiting for her to finish the story. "Anyhow, legend has it that he gave Celia a lot of jewels or gold or something when he left for the war. They couldn't find it in her things and figured she must have buried it." Eleanor glanced at her dirty hands sheepishly. "And we Wildings have been searching for it ever since."

Kelly stopped digging. "My folks got married because my mom was pregnant," she said abruptly, not looking at Eleanor. "With me."

Eleanor folded her hands around her knees, ignoring the urge to reach out and comfort Kelly. The girl's stiff spine and averted head told her Kelly wasn't ready for that.

"Does that bother you?" She kept her tone even.

"I guess so." Kelly broke her twig in half and let it fall into the dirt. "It's like it makes everything *my* fault. And it doesn't seem fair."

"No. It's a bit upside down, isn't it?" Eleanor smiled slightly. "Two grown-ups and one little baby—and the *baby* is to blame?"

Kelly frowned. "Well, that's what it feels like." Her voice had a defiant note, but her face, dappled by the morning sun and devoid of makeup, looked much younger than it had last night, more approachable.

Eleanor knew that this was the moment for Frank's famous "reflective listening," when she should simply mirror Kelly's statements, not arguing or judging but giving Kelly the right to her own feelings. But instinct told her Kelly wanted something more, and she took a chance.

"You know," she began tentatively, "if you watch, I think you'll see that people do pretty much what they want to do. They may not admit it, and they may construct some elaborate excuses for doing it. But if two intelligent grown-ups decide to make a baby and get married, I'd be willing to bet it was what they wanted all along."

As she spoke, a thought sprang unbidden into her mind. What if, the night she and Edan had made love, she had become pregnant? Would it actually have been the fulfillment of a secret desire?

She pressed her fingers together until they were white against the pink of her knees. She had to admit the answer was yes. A child would have given her something of her own, someone who wouldn't love anyone but her. And it might have tied Edan to her.

She felt herself flushing. How horrible to have to face the stupid selfish truth about herself! And yet, though it had been stupid, she still pitied that young Eleanor Wilding, who had felt so alone.

Just as she now felt sorry for Kelly. The girl sat a long time, chewing her lip, apparently considering Eleanor's words.

Finally she spoke. "You really think so?"

"Yep."

A smile twitched at one corner of Kelly's lips. "It makes people seem pretty silly," she said, "when you look at it that way."

Eleanor nodded. "But human. And we're all the same. Silly and sad—and human."

"Well, maybe." Kelly looked a little dubious, but her face was somehow lighter. "Hey, if we don't get hunting we'll never find this so-called treasure." She stood and picked up the shovel she had dropped beside the cabin. "Not that I believe for a minute we will. If there ever was a treasure, which I doubt, some dorky Wilding from a hundred years ago probably already found it and spent every penny."

Recognizing Kelly's need to change the subject, Eleanor stood up, too. She'd said enough for now. Any more would just be a lecture and fall on deaf ears.

"Oh, yeah?" She playfully wrested the shovel from Kelly's hands. "Then you'd better let me dig. You'll never find the treasure if you don't dig with a sincere heart. The legend says so."

She tromped ahead of Kelly, who was chuckling for the first time that day. "That's the Great Pumpkin legend, Eleanor. You've got your legends mixed up again."

They hadn't even decided where to dig when Nicholas, his face filthy but beaming through the grime, came racing over.

"Come on," he cried, panting and gesturing with grubby hands. He grabbed Eleanor's arm. "Come on! They found it! Edan and Gina found the treasure!"

CHAPTER FIVE

NICHOLAS LED THE WAY, scampering ahead impatiently and then racing back to urge the others to hurry so that he could show them where to go. But they didn't really need a guide. Even from across the grounds, Eleanor could see the crowd gathered beneath an oak tree, uptilted faces peering into the branches, outstretched hands pointing.

In a tree? Eleanor's stride slowed as her skepticism increased. She didn't know how intelligent or resourceful Captain Wilding had been—she had abandoned the delusion of a mystical link with him a decade ago, no matter what Edan thought—but she simply couldn't imagine anybody hiding anything valuable in an old tree.

As they got closer, the excited chatter grew louder. Apparently she was the only skeptic in the bunch; the children were fairly dancing with anticipation, and even the grown-ups had a Christmas-morning eagerness in their eyes. At the fringe of the crowd, she stopped and watched.

It was quite a show. Gina was on Edan's shoulders, her long legs dangling across his chest. Though her face was hidden in the lush spring foliage, her voice carried clearly.

"Closer to the tree, honey. I can't quite reach."

Edan edged in. Kelly green leaves showered down around his feet as Gina rustled the branches violently.

"Closer!" Gina sounded impatient, and she jabbed him gently with her heels.

Edan grimaced, but he inched closer, maneuvering around the thick roots that snaked in and out of the earth forming treacherous loops. He was wonderfully agile, his legs, bare beneath his navy shorts, gracefully masculine. His muscles bunched and rippled as he shifted his weight, and as if in answer, a muscle clenched in Eleanor's midsection. She had to look away. She stared at her feet and tried not to remember...

But, against her will, she was fifteen again, giddy with the joy of being back at Wildings for summer vacation. The sun was warm on her arms, and she was running, racing with Edan, her handsome new stepbrother, laughing delightedly because she had almost caught him. And then, without warning, she was lurching forward, the toe of her sneaker snagged on a root. She must have cried out, for Edan whirled and, keeping his balance with that spectacular athletic grace of his, caught her as she fell.

He held her tightly as they hit the ground together. The impact—and his grip—knocked the breath out of her, and she lay atop him, gasping for air. In that moment of silent panic, their eyes met—hers frightened and disoriented, his dark, concerned and somehow reassuring.

Even when her breath had painfully returned, he held her, his gaze locked with hers. His hands were hot against her shoulder blades, his hipbones unyielding beneath her thighs. And, though she was clearly safe, her body still tingled with fear, and she was the first to drop her eyes.

It wasn't until much later that she realized she had taken a second fall that day, a long and dangerous emotional plunge....

"Eek!"

The high-pitched scream broke into Eleanor's thoughts, and she started, alarmed.

A ruckus by the tree drew her attention, and she looked over just in time to see Gina slithering down Edan's torso, sputtering and fussing. Eleanor couldn't remember ever seeing the serene Gina this flustered.

"It moved," Gina gasped, squeezing Edan's shirt in two fists, as though he were single-handedly responsible for her distress. "Right under my hands, it moved. It was disgusting!"

Edan's mouth quirked. "It was probably just a beetle," he said indulgently. "It can't hurt you."

"It was not a beetle. It was slimy!" Gina's voice trembled, and her body seemed to tremble, too. She put her arm around Edan's waist. "It was awful. I'm not sticking my hand into that hole again, not for all the money in the Confederate treasury."

There was a general murmur of disappointment, and Nicholas wailed in protest. "You can't just leave it there," he fumed, scowling at Gina. "You're such a chicken." He looked at Edan for confirmation. "Girls are so stupid, aren't they? It was probably only a lizard."

Edan chuckled, but Gina clearly didn't find Nicholas at all amusing. She yanked with suppressed fury at a leaf that had caught in her hair and turned on the boy.

"Oh, yeah? Well, why don't you go get it yourself, buster?"

Nicholas squared his short sturdy legs and met Gina's wrath manfully. "Because I'm not big enough, that's why. I can't reach. It takes a grown-up, but it takes a grown-up with guts, which you haven't got.''

Gina snorted, apparently ready to do battle with her tiny critic, but Edan put his hands between them, like a referee at a prize fight.

''Okay, kids, break it up. We'll find somebody else to do it. We should have known Gina wouldn't be pleased about getting her hair all mussed, anyway.''

His smile took the sting out of his words, and Gina smoothed her hair, apparently mollified. ''I never was much of a tomboy,'' she simpered, and Eleanor could swear Gina actually batted her lashes. Good grief.

''Well, I know somebody who was,'' Edan countered, and the mischief in his voice was unmistakable. ''A first-class tomboy. Let's ask her.''

Eleanor felt a sinking sensation in the pit of her stomach, but she forced herself to look at him. As she had suspected, he was staring straight at her, laughter crinkling the corners of his eyes.

''How about it, Nellie? You're not scared of a little lizard, are you?''

Everyone was watching her. He knew, of course, that her tomboy act had been just that—an act. She was wretchedly afraid of spiders and snakes and the other creepy-crawly things that boys seemed to delight in. She always had been. But too proud, even at twenty-five, to admit it, she tilted her head and parried with a question of her own.

''Why don't you just climb up there yourself?''

His grin deepened. ''We'd decided to let one of the ladies have the honor of discovering the treasure. But I'll climb up if you like.'' He raised one brow. ''If you're scared.''

She saw the challenge in his gray eyes, a challenge she found all too familiar. *See how high I can jump, Nell— can you? See how long I can stay underwater, Nell—can you?* And in spite of herself, she felt her dander rising. Pulling her upper lip through her teeth slowly, she took a deep breath and strode through the crowd.

"Of course I'm not scared."

"Good." His smile was triumphant, and as she reached him he squatted, holding out one hand to help her onto his back.

And suddenly, with that hard tanned hand in front of her, she *was* afraid. Not of the unseen things that crawled in the trees. It was the intimacy that scared her—the way their bodies would be entwined.

But just as she had sailed her pony over the too-high bar, just as she had held her face in the murky Mississippi until her lungs were bursting, she now put her slightly clammy hand in his.

His grip tightened as though to prevent second thoughts, and he grinned at her. "Atta girl," he said softly.

She didn't bother to answer. Bracing her foot on his knee, she hoisted one leg over his broad shoulder and straddled his neck. The intimacy almost took her breath away and, teetering, she clutched his head like the pommel of a saddle, her fingers sinking into his thick sun-warmed curls.

"Careful." Reaching up with both hands, he cupped her waist and centered her weight on his shoulders. As he did, his hair snagged on the button of her shorts, and he shook his head to work it free. The muscles of her inner thighs tensed as they registered every movement he made.

She held her breath, for even breathing seemed to press her too close to him. She was starting to feel light-headed when, apparently satisfied that her balance was secure, he slid his hands down and caught her knees, placing his thumbs against the sensitive hollows behind them for a better grip.

"Up we go, then. You're looking for a little knot-hole above the third branch. Gina said she saw something shining in there, like metal."

Easily, smoothly, he rose to his feet. As the leaves closed around her, she saw the knothole, deep and dark, just over her head. But she was not as tall as Gina, and she couldn't see far enough into the hole to tell what, if anything, was hidden there.

Her fingers were still nestled in Edan's hair, but he was so steady that there was really no need to hang on. She willed her hands to move, but they ignored her instructions, as if the silky strands that encircled each finger were unbreakable bonds.

"See it?"

"Yes." The syllable was hoarse and rough. Something skittered on a branch above her.

"Can you get to it?"

"I think so." She dragged one hand free from his hair and reached up. Her fingertips barely grazed the bottom of the hole. "No, not quite."

"Lean forward."

He said it casually, as though it never occurred to him what leaning forward would mean, as though her bare thighs around his neck were a matter of indifference to him.

And so she did lean forward, stretching as far as she could. He put his hands under her feet and propped her up slightly, until she was half standing, half balancing against him. The blood rushed toward her ears in a torrent, and she shut her eyes. She could hardly bear it. She'd rather encounter a hundred crawling bugs here in this knothole than endure this aching union another moment.

Eyes still shut, she slipped her hand into the hole. Her fingers blindly searching, sliding across the musty fungus of a hundred years of darkness and finally resting on something hard. Hard, square and clearly metallic.

She grabbed the thing and whisked it out of the hole. "I got it!" Her voice shook, and she settled back onto Edan's shoulders with profound relief. She handed it down to him. "You open it."

He titled his head back, the crown of his head nudging against her stomach, forcing a painful ripple of awareness through her body. "Don't you want to?"

She gripped a branch, struggling for composure. It was ridiculous to be this aware of a man, this easily aroused, helpless to control her responses. She only prayed he couldn't tell. "You open it," she repeated stubbornly.

"Okay."

Looking down, she could see the crowd pressing forward, eager to watch the box being opened. She couldn't see Edan's hands, but she heard the rusty squeal of protesting metal as he pried the lid off.

In spite of herself, she felt her pulse accelerate. It was a small box, but clearly it had been in the tree a long time.

Suddenly his shoulders shook under her, and she realized he was chuckling.

"What?" she demanded, wishing for the first time that she had opened it herself. "What is it?"

He laughed out loud. "Marbles," he said. "Marbles and pieces of colored glass and broken shells." A fresh murmur of disappointment rumbled through the crowd. "It was someone's treasure, all right, but that someone must have been about eight years old."

Then everyone began talking at once, but Nicholas's outraged cry could be heard above the din. "No!" he exploded, his little-boy voice full of the pain of dashed hopes. He snatched the box from Edan and, after confirming that it contained nothing but old junk, flung it to the ground. "Damn it!"

"Nicholas Wilding!" His mother grabbed his arm and dragged him away. "If I ever hear you talking like that again..." Her words faded into the distance. Eleanor could see the others moving slowly away, too.

"Coming down? Or do you like it up there?"

Edan's voice was amused. Embarrassed, Eleanor let go of her branch and put her hands on her thighs.

"Well, it's a bit far to jump."

"True." Without warning, he reached up, circled her waist with his hands and, lifting her over his head, lowered her to the ground.

Her circulation must have been cut off. Her feet were on the ground, but her legs felt unsteady, as though they might not hold her up. She swayed slightly, and he pulled her to him, moving with her until his back was against the tree, and her back was against his chest.

"Disappointed?" His hands were still on her waist, and his head was close to her ear. The word was spoken softly, with a warm exhalation of breath that brushed her cheek.

"Not very." She looked across the yard at her relatives as they returned to the house. She and Edan were alone, here in the privacy of the oak tree, where the shade was cool and the air smelled like new leaves and wet earth. "I never really thought it was up there. I can't see Captain Wilding expecting his pregnant girlfriend to climb a tree to get her money."

He chuckled again, his chest moving rhythmically under her shoulder blades. "How practical you are, Nellie." He released her almost absently, and she stepped a little away, if only to show that she could.

They remained silent for a moment, she looking toward the Mississippi, he gazing over her head at the house. "Charlotte wants badly for us to find the treasure," he said finally, bringing his gaze back to her. It was somber. "I think she's really hoping there's a fortune out here."

Eleanor frowned. "Why?" It was so unlike Charlotte to indulge in fancies. Suddenly a disturbing thought occurred to her. "Edan, does she need money?"

He shook his head. "No. For now, she's fine. But she's thinking about the future. I guess she wants to know what's going to happen to Wildings when she's gone. It's a valuable piece of property. It wouldn't be the first old home that had to be sold to pay inheritance taxes."

Eleanor stiffened. Had Edan and Charlotte been discussing the terms of her will? It wouldn't surprise her. He probably knew what Charlotte's plans were, knew what was going to happen to the only home Eleanor had ever loved. This was all a cat-and-mouse game to him. Well, she wasn't going to play. Folding her arms across her chest, she asked straight out, "What is she going to do with Wildings, Edan? Who's she going to leave it to?"

A shadow swept over his face. "Who do you think she should leave it to, Eleanor?"

A knot rose in her throat, a mix of resentment and anxiety. "Don't play games, Edan. And don't patronize me. Just answer me."

One side of his mouth lifted in a smile that was somehow not pleasant. "I don't know."

She made a disgusted sound. "I don't believe that."

"It's true." He spoke without emphasis; he didn't seem to care whether she believed him or not. "But what if she did leave it to you, Nell? Would you come back to Mississippi to live? Would you finally be willing to accept money from Wildings Realty so that you could afford to keep it? Or would you just sell it?"

She squeezed her arms tighter. "I don't know. I don't know any of the details...."

"You're pale, Nellie. You're scared, aren't you? You don't even want the damn house. But you're scared to death that she's going to leave Wildings to someone else—to me, for instance."

She raised her brows, affecting surprise, though her heart was racing. "I hadn't thought of that. She has a house full of Wildings up there. Why on earth would she leave it to you?"

His one-sided smile deepened. "Maybe because none of them actually cares about this place. Maybe she knows every one of them would sell the house in a minute, take the money and run."

"I wouldn't," she said, and the plaintive note embarrassed her. She knew immediately that she had given him the opening he'd been waiting for.

"Wouldn't you?" His voice was sharp. "Seems to me running away is your specialty."

Humiliatingly, she suddenly wanted to cry. Oh, he had always known exactly how to hurt her.

"I hate you," she said, her own voice low and bitter. "I really hate you."

"So I've heard." He looked bored now, the flash of anger gone. He glanced down at the small box of colored stones at their feet. "You know, this might have been Captain Wilding's treasure, after all. He wasn't always a soldier. Once upon a time he was a little boy— and then he grew up. Everyone does."

He pulled himself erect and walked away, kicking the box with his foot as he passed it. "Everyone but you."

THE POOR ONION didn't have a chance.

"Self-righteous." Slash. "Obnoxious." Slash. "Infuriating." Slash. "Impossible, pompous—"

"Ouch!" The knife, wielded with more violence than wisdom, slashed Eleanor's thumb, and a thick line of blood seeped out of the wound. She sucked the aching spot quickly. Good thing it hadn't been a butcher knife. She was already dressed for dinner, and a cut from that would have bled all over her pink gown.

She had managed to avoid Edan all day, but her thoughts had proved more difficult to control. Helping out in the kitchen, she frequently found herself attacking a carrot or a cantaloupe with more vigor than necessary.

After several hours away from him, she had even begun to see the humor in her displaced fury. "Take that, Edan Bond," she muttered under her breath as she ripped the heart out of a head of lettuce. One of the day helpers hired to handle the reunion shot her a very strange look and sidled over to the other end of the counter.

The rest of the clan had gone on the official reunion adventure, a riverboat trip, but Eleanor hadn't felt able to face it. Trapped on a boat with Edan? Nowhere to run if his comments grew too snide? She hacked at the onion one final time. No way.

Besides, tonight's dinner was really more than the hired help could manage alone. Even the formal dining room wouldn't accommodate all the expected guests— half a dozen small tables had been set up for the youngsters on the veranda, where spilt milk wouldn't do much damage and irrepressible giggles would waft away unnoticed on the open breeze.

It felt good to be back in the big kitchen at Wildings, where she had spent some of the happiest hours of her childhood. She had rolled dough for biscuits, and when she'd looked down she could almost see, instead of her own hands, her grandmother's deft fingers covered with flour. Her grandmother, who was upstairs resting so that she would have the stamina to get through one family dinner, had once ruled this entire kitchen.

Her vision blurred, causing her to blink briskly. Well, at least Charlotte had trained Eleanor's hands to take over. She'd pounded the dough, proving herself worthy with every puff of white smoke.

Later she had lovingly wiped spots off goblets so familiar they almost broke her heart. The last time she'd seen these goblets used, her father had been alive. She remembered well how he'd poured a few drops of blood red wine into her glass. "You're too young for much," he'd said. And then he had proceeded to fill Edan's to the brim. A wobbly smile played at her lips at the memory. It had seemed like such a personal insult. She hadn't taken into account the fact that Edan was almost four years older.

What a mixed-up little girl she had been! She'd shaken her head at the distorted reflection she saw in the convex bowl of the goblet. Edan was wrong. She *had* grown up, was growing up all the time. Or was trying to, anyway. She did better when he wasn't around.

Dinner was late, giving the returning boaters an opportunity to shower and change. Edan and Gina arrived together—Eleanor heard them as they mounted the stairs, though she tried not to listen. But judging from Gina's mellow laughter, it didn't sound as if she'd had any trouble enduring Edan's company on the boat all afternoon.

But when Edan came down again he was escorting Charlotte, who looked beautiful in a long powder blue gown with lace high at her slender throat. Edan, too, was stunning in his dinner jacket, his hair still damp from his shower and appearing darker than ever.

If she didn't know, she never would have guessed they weren't related. They were clearly of a kind, both erect and poised, with an innate dignity in their bearing and a keen intelligence in their eyes. They were, at the very least, kindred in spirit.

Watching them, Eleanor felt hollow. It was as if for the first time she could truly believe that Charlotte might leave Wildings to Edan. And for the first time she could see why that might make sense.

The hollowness increased, growing into a cavern of loss. If Edan had indeed become more Charlotte's grandchild than Eleanor was, where did that leave her? And if she was not justified in hating him, what did she feel?

Charlotte stopped at the foot of the stairs. She held out her hand to Eleanor, who stood, paralyzed, in front of her.

"What a pretty dress," Charlotte said, taking Eleanor's hand and wrapping it in her thin, but somehow comforting one. "Doesn't she look beautiful, Edan?"

Eleanor stared down at her dress, a pink watered silk sheath, with a sense of surprise. She barely remembered putting it on. She'd left the kitchen late and done a whirlwind make-over.

"Thanks," she said quickly, hoping to forestall Edan's response. Honestly—why did Charlotte keep inviting Edan to compliment her? It made her feel ridiculous, like a kid on a blind date. An uncomfortable suspicion insinuated itself into her thoughts. Charlotte wasn't up to a bit of matchmaking, was she?

"Absolutely breathtaking," Edan agreed, and Eleanor winced. That was a shameless exaggeration of course, and no doubt deliberate, designed to negate the compliment altogether. Charlotte nodded, apparently pleased, and moved ahead into the dining room to greet the others.

That left Eleanor alone with Edan, whose wry smile was quite disconcerting. Had he, too, noticed Charlotte's ploy? How absurd he must find it!

He studied Eleanor's face for a long moment. "Yes. Gorgeous." He touched her jaw near her ear. "The flour is an especially nice touch."

Her hand flew to her face, which she felt turning as pink as her dress. "Sorry. I was making biscuits, and I didn't have time to redo my makeup...." She rubbed vigorously at the spot.

"Don't." He nudged her hand away. "It has a certain Cinderella pathos. Dutiful granddaughter slaving away in the kitchen all day—unloved, unappreciated."

Before she could respond, he glanced toward the dining room, where Charlotte was motioning for them to join her.

"And the real irony," he said, looking back at Eleanor, "is that Charlotte has me in mind for the part of Prince Charming. Have you noticed?"

Eleanor swallowed her anger. How smug and disdainful he was! Well, she wouldn't give him the satisfaction of showing her anger or her embarrassment. "I think you must be mistaken. Charlotte would never cast so completely against type. She knows full well that Prince Charming is a role that's just not in your repertoire."

Grinning, as though he enjoyed her attempts to quell him, he held out his arm with ostentatious courtesy. "True, but you're overlooking the obvious. We each own half of a prosperous business. Think how charming our combined incomes would be, particularly when it comes time to pay the castle taxes."

Her hand froze midway to his arm. His tone was facetious, but she heard the truth beneath his teasing. Could that be what Charlotte was hoping for?

Instinctively her eyes sought her grandmother. Charlotte was already seated at the head of the table, her frail form managing, as it always had, to dominate the long crowded room. Did Charlotte really dream that someday Eleanor and Edan would sit at the two ends of that table? Together. As owners...partners...

Eleanor's breath caught. Charlotte couldn't know how impossible that dream was. And she must never know that it had once been Eleanor's dream, too.

"They're waiting." Edan's arm was still crooked, and drawing a shaky breath, Eleanor slipped her hand inside his elbow and let him propel her into the other room.

For Eleanor, the dinner passed in a muffled black-and-white dream. She and Edan sat on either side of Charlotte, and occasionally Eleanor would glance up to see Edan staring at her, his dark eyes speculative. His lips would move silently, forming the command, "Eat." And in unthinking obedience, she would raise her fork to her mouth. But she never tasted a thing.

Dishes appeared and disappeared like props in a magic show, until coffee cups steamed in front of them and dinner was almost over. She lifted her cup and drank deeply of its bitter contents, thankful that she would soon be alone where she could think.

"Attention, children, attention." Charlotte was standing, and everyone looked her way. Eleanor looked, too, and something in Charlotte's eager smile made her skin prickle.

"I have an announcement to make," Charlotte said. "One that will probably shock you."

"You always shock us, Charley," Eleanor's great-uncle Ned called from the far end of the table. There was a ripple of laughter.

"Thank you, sir. I certainly try." Charlotte bowed her head in mock gratitude. "To continue. I know this will seem strange. Since some of you will probably say I've grown senile to even consider such a thing, let me address that at the beginning."

Her gaze fell on Eleanor. "For the record, I'm not losing touch with reality. Quite the opposite. Sometimes I think I must have been born senile, and grown more clearheaded with every passing year. However, I'm old enough to have finally learned what is important and what isn't. Who's important and who isn't. I used to believe in status and money, in convention and order. Now I know those things are worthless. Now I believe in love and laughter and dreams.''

Eleanor's eyes burned, but she held back the hot tears. She couldn't meet Charlotte's soft blue gaze.

''To get to the point. I've been having a hard time deciding how to write my will. I know what the lawyers tell me to do. I know what common sense tells me to do. But my heart is confused.''

Eleanor twisted her hands in her lap, pressing her fingers together until bone ground against bone. Her cut ached and started to bleed again slightly.

''So I've decided to let Captain Wilding decide.''

''What?'' The word was spoken almost in unison, up and down the table. ''Who?''

Charlotte's smile was full of mischievous delight. She had always loved being unpredictable. Eleanor risked peeking at Edan. To her surprise, he looked thoroughly amused, his dark eyes twinkling.

''Captain Wilding,'' Charlotte continued, her voice firm and brooking no dispute. ''I've decided that if anyone finds his treasure here this week, then that person will inherit Wildings.''

CHAPTER SIX

"GOOD HEAVENS, CHARLEY! You must be joking!"

Uncle Ned's voice was the loudest, but the same sentiment—articulated with varying degrees of tact—was expressed by almost everyone at the table.

Only Eleanor, who was too shocked to speak, and Edan, who apparently wasn't surprised at all, were quiet. After her first glimpse of his amused grin, Eleanor avoided Edan's gaze, though she could feel him staring at her.

"Why must I be joking?" Charlotte drew herself up to her full height and glared at Uncle Ned. "I have no children—both my boys are gone. Instead I have one granddaughter, one step-grandson, several nieces and nephews, and assorted and sundry cousins and in-laws. How could I choose among you? I don't think you could cut Wildings into that many pieces."

A rueful smile played at the edges of her mouth, though she continued to fix a stern look on her nephew. "Besides, not one of you had the good sense to become a millionaire. If we don't find the treasure, Wildings could easily end up being sold for taxes. Or worse, Ned, you'll get hold of it and turn it into the Rebel Yell Hotel."

"Never," Uncle Ned maintained indignantly. "Hotels are too damn much work."

Little Nicholas, whose mouth was technically still too full of coconut pie to speak, licked his meringue mustache and scowled at Charlotte.

"This isn't fair," he mumbled around the pie. "I want the treasure, but I don't want this old house. It's too spooky. I like our house in Pittsburgh better."

Nicholas's mother gripped his shoulder warningly, but Charlotte laughed.

"That's all right, Nicholas. If you find the treasure, you can give the house to one of the others, as long as you promise to help pay the taxes."

"Good." Nicholas surveyed the dinner guests. His eyes stopped at Edan. "I'll give it to Edan. He's not afraid of ghosts one bit."

Edan winked at the little boy. "Thanks," he said. "You can come visit if it's okay with the ghost."

"Can I come, too?" Gina purred. Receiving Edan's nod, she turned to Charlotte, her Cheshire-cat grin smug. "I think it's a super idea. But are you sure it doesn't give Eleanor an unfair advantage? After all, she's the only one who ever actually saw our friendly ghost. Maybe he told her where the treasure's buried."

The laughter that echoed through the room bewildered Eleanor. No sign of tension, competition, greed—obviously none of these people particularly yearned to inherit Wildings. This was just a whimsical adventure to them. They probably thought of Wildings as the family white elephant, more trouble than it was worth. Was she the only one who thought of it as harbor and haven?

"Come on, Gina," she said, striving for the bantering tone that would make her sound like the others. "Won't you guys ever let me live that down? I was only fifteen, for heaven's sake."

"Sorry." Edan laced his hands behind his head and stretched. "No statute of limitations on the sins of youth."

Kelly, who had been silent during the entire exchange, clearly didn't like Edan's tone, for she jumped to Eleanor's defense.

"That's dumb," she said, glaring at Edan and Gina, who were still chuckling. "Of course the ghost didn't tell her. Because if he had she would have dug the treasure up then and there."

Edan cocked one brow at Eleanor. "Good point," he said. "She wouldn't have waited ten whole years to show this doubting Thomas that she had been right all along. She would have loved to throw a fistful of doubloons smack in my face."

Everyone laughed at that. The years of feuding between Eleanor and Edan had not gone unnoticed by the reunion clan.

Kelly frowned defensively. "Phooey," she muttered. "She wouldn't have wasted the time, would you, Eleanor? She would have gone out and spent it on jewelry and clothes and stuff."

Nicholas, the only one too young to understand the undercurrents of the conversation, wriggled out from his mother's restraining grasp.

"Yuck," he said with feeling. "Clothes! I bet she would've bought a car. A red Lamborghini, with black racing stripes, right, Eleanor?"

Little boys. Eleanor couldn't help smiling. "I might have, honey. They're really neat."

Gina tickled Edan's rib cage. "And then she would have driven it back to Wildings and ran it slap over you."

Amid the general laughter Eleanor met Edan's eyes. He winked at her, much as he had winked at Nicholas earlier.

"Don't give Eleanor any ideas. If she finds the treasure first, she still may do that."

Uncle Ned cleared his throat. Though he was the family clown at every Wildings' reunion, he was a respected lawyer in Baton Rouge the rest of the year, so he was the first to return to reality.

"Okay. It's fun, I'll grant you that. But what if we don't find it, Charley?" He downed the dregs of his coffee in one gulp and wiped his lips purposefully. "Then what will you do?"

Charlotte let her gaze fall softly on Eleanor and then on Edan. "Well," she said slowly, "I guess I'll just have to think of something else."

AT MIDNIGHT, dishes done and guests seen safely into their cars or bedrooms, Eleanor tapped lightly on her grandmother's door.

"Come in." Charlotte sounded irritable, but when Eleanor opened the door, the old woman smiled. "Oh, it's you. Thank goodness. All night long I've been entertaining a parade of the most annoying busybodies I've ever laid eyes on." Marking her page with her reading glasses, she put the book she'd been reading on the bedside table. "And that's saying something, considering I used to chair the bake sale with that odious Lavinia Bishop every year."

Eleanor grinned. "Lavinia Bishop used to say the same about you, as I recall," she teased as she sat on the bed, sinking into the white satin comforter.

She glanced at Charlotte's book. A fat bestseller, written by one of the current masters of horror.

"Gran," she scolded, eyeing the alarming monster on the cover. "This?"

Charlotte sniffed. "Why not? Just because I'm eighty-six doesn't mean I want to lie in bed all day and read Tennyson or Melville or some other worthy drone. I'm old, not dead."

"You might die of fright."

"I will not, and if you came in here to nag me, then you can scoot along to bed like the rest of them." Charlotte pulled the covers up and frowned down her aristocratic nose at Eleanor. It was a maneuver that once had intimidated little Nell thoroughly. Now, as an adult, Eleanor could clearly see the twinkle in Charlotte's eyes.

"Okay!" She held her hands palms up in surrender, then smoothed the quilt around Charlotte's shoulders. "How are you feeling?"

"Fine." Meeting Eleanor's skeptical look, Charlotte shrugged. "Well, I'm a little tired. It was a long night. And your Uncle Ned ... Honestly, handling Ned must have been the thirteenth labor of Hercules. I finally told him to take all that hot air and blow himself home."

"Pontificating again?" Eleanor smiled. "What about?"

"About the treasure hunt, of course. Most 'damned unconventional thing' I've ever done, he says." Charlotte raised her brows, presenting a serene expression that Eleanor knew meant mischief. "But I reminded him of a couple of other things I've done through the years, and he had to admit he was mistaken." She let a smile peep through. "That's the good thing about being eccentric all your life. Then if you do get senile no one can tell."

"You're not senile, Gran."

"No," Charlotte agreed placidly, "I'm not." She met Eleanor's troubled gaze. "But tell me the truth, honey. You're not sure about this, either, are you?"

Eleanor picked at a loose thread in the coverlet. "Not entirely," she began. "It's just that . . . there probably isn't any treasure, you know, Gran. Wildings have been dreaming about it and looking for it for at least a hundred years." She wrinkled her nose. "Don't you think we'd have found it by now if it exists?"

Sighing heavily, Charlotte shook her head. "You disappoint me, Eleanor. I thought you were the only true believer around here. In fact, I'm quite counting on you to find it."

Eleanor groaned. "Oh, Gran—"

Charlotte sat up straighter, and her gaze was level. "Would you like to inherit Wildings?"

"Gran, I—"

"I know you have a life out in California now, but I always thought you were the only one who really understood this house. Really felt something for it. Was I wrong?"

Shaking her head, Eleanor tried to think what to say. If she poured out her intense love for Wildings, wouldn't she be doing just what Edan had accused her of? Trying to wheedle Charlotte into leaving the house to her? And if she did inherit Wildings, would her income be enough to take care of it? Exactly how much *would* inheritance taxes be? She didn't even know what the property was worth. And besides, she couldn't bear the idea of Charlotte dying. The jumbled thoughts, bumping around in her mind, created a miserable logjam, and she couldn't speak at all.

"What is it, Eleanor?" Charlotte took Eleanor's hand. "Does the house hold too many bad memories?"

"No. No, that's not it." Suddenly Eleanor's eyes stung, and her voice was tight. "Some are . . . hard, but most of my memories are wonderful." She looked at her grandmother, tears trembling in her eyes, ready to fall if she so much as blinked. "Even some of the memories that hurt are special. Important. Does that sound crazy?"

Smiling, Charlotte relaxed against the pillows. "Sounds like love to me."

A deep voice at the door broke in. "What does?"

Eleanor jerked her head up at the sound, and the precariously balanced tears spilled over, hot on her cheeks. She whisked both hands to her face, dashing the wetness away with hurried fingers. How much had he heard?

Charlotte greeted Edan with much more equanimity. "We're discussing the complicated nature of love," she said comfortably, patting the empty side of the bed. "Want to join us?"

"Sounds fascinating." Edan moved around the bed and sat down. He had taken off his dinner jacket, and his tie hung loose around his unbuttoned collar. Eleanor found herself staring at his bronzed neck, at the muscles that rose from his shoulders and disappeared into the shadow of his strong jaw.

Her stomach tightened at the memory of riding those shoulders, and she shifted nervously. She dragged her gaze away from his neck and up to his face. That didn't help. She looked at her grandmother, instead.

"It's a little late for a heavy philosophical discussion," Eleanor said airily, hoping Edan would think he had interrupted a purely academic conversation. "Why don't I go now and let you and Edan have a few minutes together before you go to sleep?"

She started to rise, but Charlotte held her hand tightly. "Stay," the old woman said, and there was a hint of need in her voice that Eleanor had never heard there before. She stayed.

"Edan usually reads to me at night when my eyes get too tired," Charlotte said. "Stay and listen. It won't be long. I always fall asleep right away."

Edan laughed. "How flattering! I won't use *you* for a reference."

Charlotte harrumphed as she fluffed her pillows and settled herself comfortably. "Don't fish for compliments, son. You know you're *trying* to put me to sleep." Turning to Eleanor, she made a face. "He reads fine, but he won't read the books *I* like. He always picks some stuffy classic. I go to sleep in self-defense."

"Well, if your tastes weren't so ghoulish..." Edan pulled a thick paperback from the night-table drawer. "Now, be still and listen."

Eleanor smiled inwardly at the title. *War and Peace*— Edan really was trying to put Charlotte to sleep. And it worked. After only a few minutes Charlotte's eyes closed, and her breathing became slow and even.

And yet, Eleanor had never felt more awake. Even if Edan was reading the telephone book, how could anyone go to sleep? His voice was wonderful, unaffectedly elegant with a purity of tone that made Eleanor feel she could listen to it forever. A tingling awareness pricked all her senses to a high pitch. The deep timbre of his voice had an effect like feathers brushing across her aroused nerve endings, and she felt goose bumps from her temples to her toes.

It was difficult to sit still. She barely heard the words he read. It was as if he spoke a foreign language, but spoke it so beautifully that every syllable stimulated, every sentence inflamed. Blood pounded in her throat, and her hands crushed the white satin coverlet in a fevered grip.

Finally she couldn't take it anymore. Though it seemed as impossible as dancing through quicksand, she knew she had to get up, had to stretch and calm her coiled muscles, had to walk away from the touch of his voice.

He didn't look up. The words continued to flow even as she stood up and crossed the room. Ignoring them, ignoring the way they seemed to follow her, enticing her back with soft unseen fingers of sound, she opened the French doors and stepped out onto the balcony.

Careful to shut the door behind her, she drank in the cool silence thirstily. She went to the ballustrade and leaned against a pillar, staring down. She couldn't see the ground; the balcony seemed to float on a cloudy river of mist. Weak moonlight picked out the strands of moss that hung like drooping flags above a becalmed ship, but left the rest of the world in near darkness.

She should have felt at peace, but she couldn't relax. She was too aware of every inch of her body. Breathing deeply, she tried to exhale the tension. It didn't work.

When she heard the French doors open behind her, the soft click shot through her like a bullet. She shut her eyes, riding the painful swell of sensation until it passed.

When she opened them again, Edan was standing beside her.

"I take it you're not a *War and Peace* fan, either?"

"Not quite." She tried to smile. "Inspired choice, though. It works better than a sleeping pill, doesn't it?"

"It always did for me." He hitched one leg up onto the balustrade, and the movement brought him closer. His thigh was only inches from her stomach, and her abdominal muscles contracted in response. "When my parents first got divorced I had trouble sleeping. My mother used to sit there for hours, reading Cooper, Stevenson, all the children's classics, but I wouldn't go to sleep. Then one night in desperation she put away *Treasure Island* and brought out *War And Peace*." He chuckled. "I never had any trouble again."

In spite of her discomfort, Eleanor laughed. "How old were you?"

"Six."

Eleanor tried to picture it—Edan as a little boy, his black hair damp from his bath, his gray eyes heavy as they fought sleep. Small, vulnerable, troubled by nightmares. But it was difficult to imagine Edan that way. He was too much a man, too completely in control. There was nothing boyish about those broad shoulders, nothing vulnerable about his firm jaw and appraising gaze. There never had been.

Maybe that was why she hadn't realized how difficult his childhood might have been. Because he was older than she, and so competent and confident, she hadn't quite believed he was ever a child. She saw now that she had mythicized him—imagining somehow that he had sprung fully grown onto the earth, perhaps astride his black stallion, galloping out of the heavens and into her life.

In hindsight the idea seemed ridiculous, but it was no wonder that she had been hopelessly confused—loving and hating him simultaneously. The fantasy had conferred such power on him. She hadn't been able to see past it to the truth, couldn't see that he was just a good-looking boy who had become an overachiever to compensate for the loss of his father.

She shifted, trying to put distance between her tense stomach and his relaxed thigh. She hadn't known it then, but she knew it now. Why didn't that knowledge make it easier? He wasn't a god or a devil; he was only a man. So why was she still breathless whenever he stood this close to her?

She backed away, feeling suddenly trapped between the cold pillar at her back and the warm body in front of her.

Her breathing was shallow, and registering it, his eyes narrowed. "Are you all right?"

Nodding, she searched for something to say. "Were you really just six? I didn't realize your parents divorced when you were so young."

He slanted her a wry look. He probably wasn't surprised that she hadn't known. He'd always said she was the most self-absorbed person he'd ever met. "Tony's parents were getting divorced about then, too. That was rather lucky for both of us. We used to talk about it a lot—we could tell each other things we couldn't tell our parents."

She nodded, understanding. Tony had been Edan's best friend. "How is Tony? Do you ever see him?"

Even before his expression changed, she realized her mistake. Lord, couldn't she say *anything* innocent? Was every word in her vocabulary laden with the guilt of the past? Would she never finish paying for the mistakes she made years ago?

"He's all right, I guess." His voice was bitter. "He went bankrupt last year, and now he works for us. I guess you hadn't heard."

"No." Charlotte hadn't written her about it. Poor Tony. He had developed a drinking problem as a teenager, and apparently he was still suffering. "I didn't know. I'm so sorry."

"Are you really?" The sarcasm in his voice was palpable. This wasn't the deep and beautiful tone he'd used while reading to Charlotte. "That certainly surprises me."

"Edan..." Eleanor put her hands to her temples, pressing against the throbbing. In the face of such undying resentment, what could she say? Oh, it was hopeless to think they could start over. From the moment she'd met Edan, she had been so awful, such a mean-spirited little fool. No wonder he hated her. She hated herself whenever she remembered.

The fiasco with Tony had probably been the most unforgivable. It had happened the first summer she'd come home from boarding school. She had nursed her broken heart, her resentments and her betrayals all year. Though she had loved Edan, he'd completely rejected her. Somehow, she had vowed as she huddled over her Latin declensions, somehow she would make him pay.

Tony's drinking problems had just been discovered, and her father had forbidden Edan to see his friend. So when Eleanor had seen Edan and Tony together, an idea had taken root in the fertile soil of angry self-pity. She'd seen Edan slipping Tony a packet that she'd decided was full of money. That had been proof enough.

She went to her father that night and told him that Edan was disobeying him, that he was still befriending Tony and even giving him money. Remembering that scene all these years later, her face flushed painfully. Her father had been furious with Edan at first, but Edan had quietly stood his ground. Tony was his friend, and he would not abandon a friend who needed him. Eleanor couldn't help admiring Edan's quiet courage. And amazingly her father had relented, even admitting he had been wrong, which was unheard of, and inviting Tony to dinner.

A happy ending all around. Except that Edan had never forgiven her. And he had minced no words. She would never forget the names he had called her. . . .

"Edan." She tried again. "Please. I know I was wrong, terribly wrong, about Tony. I know you were right to stick up for him. I just didn't think—"

"Think? Of course you didn't. You never considered how your antics might be hurting other people."

Gripping the cold balustrade, she forced down her humiliation. This had to be said. "No, I didn't. And I've spent a lot of years regretting it." She looked at him, at his dark narrowed eyes. "I know how spiteful it was. It was stupid and selfish and cruel. I want you to know *I* know that. And I want you to know I'm sorry."

There. It was done. Swallowing hard, she turned away and stared out into the opaque night. It wouldn't change anything. His resentment ran too deep to be touched by a simple apology. And yet she felt better for having said it.

Frank had helped her to see that she couldn't just run away from her mistakes. She had to face them, acknowledge them, prove to herself that she had grown beyond them. Whether Edan forgave her, whether or not he even liked her, wasn't the point. She had to like herself.

He didn't answer for a long time. Out of the corner of her eye she could see that he'd turned his head, too, and seemed to be watching something in the mist.

She shut her eyes, intensely aware of the sound of his breathing, his faint masculine scent, the warmth that emanated from his body toward hers.

As the silence lengthened, she opened her eyes again and tilted her head just enough to glance at him. The misty moonlight formed a cold aura around his head, and his profile was so still it might have been carved from marble. And yet she felt warmth where his thigh brushed her skirt. His face might be unforgiving, but something more human, more yielding, coursed through his body.

She moved toward him and touched his face tentatively, as if trying to reach him where words couldn't go. It was warm, too, and seemed to grow warmer under her fingers.

Emboldened, she spoke. "I am sorry, Edan. Really I am."

Finally he looked at her. "Are you?" The words sounded almost indifferent.

"Yes." Frustrated, she put her hands on his chest. "Yes, damn it! I'm sorry. But it was so long ago. I was only sixteen. Can't we ever put it behind us?"

He glanced at her pale hands and then up at her face. "I don't know."

"We could try." Taking his hand, she looked back toward the French doors. Charlotte appeared to be sleeping. "Grandmother wants us to be friends. I think she worries about it. I really believe that if we weren't always feuding she'd like to leave Wildings to the two of us. And if she's truly not well, maybe we should try..."

His brows contracted sharply. He followed her gaze, looking into the large, dimly lit bedroom where Charlotte lay. Then he whipped his head back to face her.

"Is that what all this sweetness and light is about? Are we putting on a show for Charlotte?" He grabbed her chin with both hands and pulled her face up to his. Shocked by the flashing anger she saw in his eyes, she drew a deep breath.

"N-no," she said, stumbling over her words, unable to move her lips properly with his hands pressing so hard. "No, of course not—"

"Like hell we're not. Wildings. It's always Wildings with you, isn't it? You want Charlotte to think we're *friends*. She wants more than that. So if we're going to put on a show, let's do it right."

Before she could speak, his lips were on hers, hot, seeking. His hands went around her, yanking her toward him, pulling her onto the balls of her feet. Tilting into him, helplessly on tiptoe, she could remain standing only if he wanted her to.

She felt his anger, as her sensitive breasts were crushed painfully against his chest and she thought her back might snap where his hands imprisoned her. She dug furiously at his shoulders with the heels of her hands, but he was too strong, too determined, and she couldn't gain an inch of freedom. Tears scalded her closed lids, held back by a pride that was tougher than pain.

And then, somehow, the kiss changed. It began as a minute lessening of pressure. Her struggling hands stilled as she became more aware of the fullness of his lips, began to perceive them as warm and probing, instead of hard and assaulting. His embrace changed, too. His fingers softened, moved, began to stroke. His hands slipped down, slowly, achingly, until they cupped the round thrust of her bottom, pressing upward.

As she met the hard contours of his body, sweet nectar spilled through her veins, and her own hands slid numbly up around his neck, all fight forgotten as the pain was completely transformed into a piercing pleasure.

Her pent-up tears fell innocently, and no new tears followed. She didn't want to cry. She wanted instead to moan, to beg, call out his name. His hands pushed harder, and a dizzying spiral of need twirled through her where their bodies met. He shifted her slowly, guiding her pelvis in small tormenting circles against him until she thought she could not bear it.

Still his mouth held hers, and once again the kiss became a blind seeking, a hungry foraging, an urgent melding. Her fingers twitched uselessly, pulling at his shirt, fists opening and shutting in unconscious rhythm. She wanted him. *Now*.

But then he pulled away.

She stared uncomprehendingly, her breath coming in short labored gasps, her blood pounding in her ears. Her legs wobbled, her feet unaccustomed to the burden of supporting her body, and she clutched the railing for support. The mist touched her wet swollen lips curiously.

"Very good, Nellie." Edan's lips were swollen, too, but they were twisted in a cruel grin. "Very convincing."

Unable to believe what her ears told her he had said, she shook her head. A sharp pain rammed into her midsection, and she covered her stomach with her arm, fighting the need to double over. "No." She shook her head again. "No."

"Oh, yes," he said, still smiling. "It was quite a performance." He glanced through the French doors. "I only hope Charlotte didn't sleep through it all. It was really award-winning quality.''

Tapping his hand to his forehead in a contemptuous salute, he walked away. Frustration hammering at her insides, she watched in disbelief as the swirling mist opened for him, slid gray fingers over his broad shoulders and down his tapering back and finally swallowed him up.

CHAPTER SEVEN

SOMEHOW, EVENTUALLY, she must have slept, for she awoke early the next morning with a pounding headache, scratchy eyes and tangled sheets wound around her leg like a thick white snake.

She squinted at the gray light under the curtains; it was probably just after dawn. She straightened the bedclothes and tried to sleep again, but it was impossible. Memories of last night, once awakened, couldn't be banished, and her headache grew worse by the minute.

Shoving the covers aside, she stood up. Maybe she couldn't control her mind, but she certainly didn't have to lie there and let her thoughts do as they pleased. She yanked on the drapery cord, the traverse mechanism zipping open with an indignant whine, then she swung wide the French doors and stepped out onto the balcony.

Immediately her misery abated. Wildings at dawn had the peaceful beauty of an enchanted forest, trees lit with a green-gold glow, grass sprinkled with the silver glitter of dew. High in a magnolia tree a lone warbler called out, and Eleanor's headache began to subside. She shut her eyes slowly, drinking in the cool blossom-sweet air, reveling in the magic of Wildings.

Back inside, she dressed quickly and quietly in jeans and a sweater, then made her way to the stables. She was ridiculously careful not to make any noise, as though doing so would break the lovely spell.

Shadow, Edan's black stallion, must have sensed her approach. Long before she saw him, she heard his whinny of welcome.

"Hi, there," she whispered as Shadow nudged her cheek. She stroked his glossy throat, wishing she had a treat for him. "I've missed you."

Movement in the next stall told her Shadow's only companion, Sweetpea, had recognized her voice, too. Giving Shadow a final pat, Eleanor moved on, eager to see the horse that once had been hers. Sweetpea thrust her graceful muzzle as far out of the stall as she could, and Eleanor smiled, touched. She had been a terrible horsewoman, but apparently Sweetpea didn't hold that against her.

"Hi," she said. Sweetpea didn't look any older. Her black eyes were still bright and curious, her neck still proudly arched, her mane still a glowing auburn against her creamy butternut coat.

Eleanor leaned against the mare's cheek. She was such a dear creature. She'd always seemed to understand Eleanor's embarrassment when her father had come to watch her riding lessons. Sometimes Eleanor imagined that Sweetpea would give an extra effort, canter more smoothly, step more cleanly, to help Eleanor impress him. Not that it had ever worked.

"Why, if it isn't the Princess and the Pea!"

For a split second the voice frightened her; she had been so sure she was alone. Sweetpea, too, started, jerking her head away with a snort. But it was only Edan, sauntering toward her from the far side of the stables, a saddle in his hand and a half grin on his wide mouth.

"Good morning," Eleanor said stiffly, reaching up to soothe Sweetpea's muzzle. How dared he look so fresh this morning? Hadn't last night's scene disturbed his rest at all? He must have come straight from the showers—his hair was damp, his dark eyes sparkling. And those jeans . . . they were so old they had memorized every muscle in his body, and yet he looked simply wonderful.

"Princess and the Pea. Funny—I'd forgotten how you used to call us that."

"Really?" He tossed the saddle across the door of Shadow's stall. "I'm shocked. I thought you kept a list of grievances next to your heart at all times."

"Sorry," she said with an overly bright smile. "You must be thinking of your own list."

"No." His grin deepened. "I've committed mine to memory."

Looking away, Eleanor declined to respond. She wasn't going to indulge in this juvenile bickering any longer. He had always enjoyed fencing with her verbally, probably because he had always won. His wit had never waned, and she would end up sputtering something lame and incoherent about how she hated him.

"Going for a ride?" She glanced down at the saddle. It looked like the same one he'd been using forever.

He nodded, raising his brows. "Join me?"

Her stomach clenched. Hadn't he guessed she didn't like to ride? Actually that was an understatement. Riding—even riding the placid Sweetpea—felt like being strapped to a time bomb. And yet . . .

"Sure." Where had *that* come from? She could almost see Frank frowning. Hadn't she learned *anything?* Back at the center, it had sounded so easy. Take responsibility for your own decisions, Eleanor. No one can force you to do anything you don't feel good about. But here she was, forcing herself into a stupid game of chicken that only she knew they were playing.

As Edan saddled both horses and led them outside, she considered a dozen ways to get out of riding, from pleading sick to simply bolting. But her mouth wouldn't work and her legs wouldn't move, and before she knew it he was holding Sweetpea's reins and gesturing for her to mount. She did so with a sickly smile.

Watching Edan mount Shadow, she clung to the reins and clung with equal desperation to the hope that Sweetpea had aged into a tired old slowpoke. "Steady now," she murmured, as much to herself as to the horse.

No such luck. As soon as Edan clicked his soft command to Shadow, both horses took off with the enthusiasm of two-year-olds. With Sweetpea's muscular body rippling beneath her, Eleanor squeezed her knees until her thighs ached, gripped the reins until her knuckles whitened, and prayed.

Gradually, though, when she didn't fall off and Sweetpea didn't go careening into the Mississippi, her fear subsided, and she accustomed herself to the rocking rhythm. Maybe she'd survive this, after all.

They reached the limits of the Wilding property quickly and cantered across the open country to the north. The pines and live oaks, magnolias and dogwood that had been passing by in a blur slowed and separated into individual trees as Eleanor relaxed. She almost began to enjoy herself. Though the sun was higher now, and warm against her face, it still was a beautiful morning.

But it was difficult to concentrate on the beauty of the spring foliage with Edan just ahead of her. She found herself staring at him, entranced by how he and his horse seemed to move as one, both strong and graceful, both fluid and masculine. Edan's strong back was outlined beneath his shirt as he leaned forward, following the line of the horse.

She shouldn't have let her mind wander. Sensing that Eleanor was not in charge, Sweetpea took her lead from Shadow, and when Edan stepped up the pace Eleanor found herself dragged along in his wake. The canter became a gallop, the horses flying faster and faster, until the passing azaleas were only smears of fiery color and the sun flickered like a strobe between the treetops.

Eleanor's mouth was suddenly so dry she couldn't swallow, and her heart rose in her throat. In front of her, with cruel certainty, she saw the hedge Edan intended to jump. Sweetpea was heading inexorably toward it, ready to leap. Eleanor groaned, but the wind stole the sound away.

Though she had never actually fallen, she had been plagued by nightmares of this scene ever since her first riding lesson. The horse beneath her, out of control; Edan in front of her, daring her, mocking her... She had always awakened crying, head throbbing, heart hammering. She was crying now, though the rushing air dried the tears on her cheeks.

The hedge seemed to be hurtling toward her. Her field of vision narrowed to one spot of unnatural clarity, and she saw Edan and Shadow, poised, ready to spring. Her feet and hands, even her mind, went numb. She was next, and she could do nothing to stop it.

As Shadow cleared the hedge, a miracle happened. The mind she couldn't control gave an order to the hands she couldn't feel, and somehow she jerked convulsively on the reins. Confused, Sweetpea checked her stride and swerved aside just as they approached the hedge. Eleanor felt her knee brush the branches as they turned.

The relief was so violent she couldn't stop shuddering. Gasping, she slid from the saddle and, holding the reins in one trembling hand, stumbled toward the thick stand of oaks that ran alongside the field. Pressing her forehead into a tree, she waited for the shaking to pass.

She heard Shadow's easy canter as Edan doubled back, but she didn't lift her face from the tree. She couldn't stop shaking and she couldn't stop crying and she just wanted him to go away.

"What's wrong?" Edan sounded impatient and even Shadow seemed irritated by the delay, prancing in restless circles.

"Nell?" When she didn't answer, she heard him drop to the ground. Then his hands were on her shoulders, pressing hard enough to make her turn. "Nell, what's wrong?"

"I didn't want to jump." She glared at him through her tears. "I didn't want to. And I didn't have to." Her tone was shrill, but she couldn't help it. Her throat was still too tight to permit normal speech. "You couldn't make me jump."

As her voice broke on the last sentence, he eased her into his arms. "What are you talking about? Of course you don't have to jump." He smoothed hair away from her damp face, picking out a piece of bark. "No one was trying to *make* you do anything."

He might have been talking to a child. Yet surprisingly, his tone didn't offend her. Instead, she wanted more than anything to bury her face in his shoulder and let her tears flow freely. But that would never do. Cry

in front of Edan? Ask, however indirectly, for his help
and support? Horrified at her own weakness, she tried
to pull away.

"Let go," she said in a strangled voice. "Let me go."

"Shh." He was whispering, his lips against her hair.
"Relax."

"I want to go home," she said, holding herself as
stiffly as her shaking would allow.

"Not yet. Tell me what happened back there."

She met his gaze stubbornly. "Nothing. I just didn't
want to jump, that's all." As he searched her eyes, obviously waiting for more, she clenched her teeth. She
knew she couldn't go on sounding like a sulky child, but
the truth was so embarrassing. "I'm *afraid* to jump.
Okay? I'm afraid of horses—I always have been. And
I'm scared to death of jumping."

His brows contracted sharply, and his hands twitched
on her arms. "You are? You've never said so before. I
must have seen you jump a hundred times."

"Well, that's a hundred times you've seen me scared
to death, then," she said acidly. Venting her anger
seemed to help the shaking, at least a little. She was
more accustomed to being angry with Edan than she
was to being honest. But his eyes were probing, and she
knew he wouldn't accept less than the truth. "I didn't
tell anyone," she admitted reluctantly, "because I was
embarrassed."

"Why?" He actually looked surprised. "A lot of
people are afraid to ride. It's hardly a serious flaw."

Of course *he* wouldn't understand, he who was born
with all the right talents, all the requisite confidence.
He'd probably never felt inadequate in his life. She felt
the bracing anger rise, burning away the embarrassment.

"My father thought it was. He already thought girls were useless, and I wasn't going to give him another reason to be disappointed in me. So I rode. And I jumped." She looked away. "And I was scared to death."

He tilted his head toward the open meadow, where the horses were quietly grazing. "Even of Sweetpea?"

"Even of Sweetpea." She looked back at him, her jaw set, still feeling defensive. "I know it's ridiculous. It's a phobia. I've seen a dozen kids struggling with phobias since I've been at the center. Scared to swim, even in a baby pool. Scared of bugs, even harmless ones. Scared of the dark, even in their own rooms. It's ridiculous, but it's real."

"What's ridiculous," he said, "is your jumping and riding all those years. What's ridiculous is your refusing to tell us about it."

"Well, I'm telling you now." She had to admit she knew what he meant. Lots of people had phobias; everyone had fears. But she hadn't trusted her family to love her in spite of her weakness. She'd let her insecurity lead her into constant misery.

"Anyway, just now I *didn't* jump. I may still be afraid of horses, but at least I'm not afraid of your knowing about it." She smiled, a mere ghost of a smile. "Surely that constitutes progress."

He didn't return the smile. His thumbs rubbed the bare skin of her arms as he stared at her. "Poor Nell." He shook his head slightly. "I didn't know."

Annoyance flashed again, sparking dangerously out of the combustible mix of emotions her fear had stirred in her. "Why should you have known?" He'd always thought he knew everything about her; he'd labeled her selfish, devious, spoiled and careless. "As much as it may shock you, you didn't have me *completely* figured out."

"It doesn't shock me." His eyes went several shades darker. "I always knew my vision wasn't quite clear where you were concerned."

"What does that mean?" Her words were terse, more terse than the situation seemed to call for. But her pulse was speeding up again, reacting to something subtly disturbing—something in his eyes, in the warmth of his fingers.

Still unsmiling, he moved his hands up to her face slowly. The movement had a tightly harnessed tension, as if an accelerator and a brake were being applied simultaneously. His fingers slid into her hair, just above her ears, where her pulse beat against them in a thick heavy rhythm.

"It means," he said, and his voice had the same growling tension, "I never could see straight for wanting you."

At first she couldn't speak. Somewhere deep inside her the shaking started again, so deep it felt as though her soul were shifting. And yet, why should this surprise her? It wasn't as if she was physically unattractive. Other men had wanted her, blatantly, and sometimes persistently. But Edan had always seemed remote and unreachable, especially in the long years since that night in the gazebo. Sometimes she had thought he disliked even looking at her.

"You wanted me?" The words were stupid, a vacant echoing that didn't communicate any of the complicated emotions sweeping through her, but they were all she could manage.

His hands clenched, twisting into her hair. "From the moment I met you."

She tried to turn away, to evade the intensity of his voice, his face, his hands. But the primitive sensations caused by the fingers tangled in her hair held her hostage.

Unable to escape physically, she tried to escape into a wry detachment.

"I was only fifteen when you met me, just a fifteen-year-old tomboy," she said, but her voice wasn't wry at all. It was throaty, shaky, and spoke of her inner turmoil more eloquently than words. "How could you—"

"Exactly." He broke in violently, stepping closer. "How could I? You were so young, so unaware of things like that." His fingers tightened more, and he pulled her face nearer his. "So young... My new sister... And your father, thrilled with his new family, trusting me completely. I nearly went mad."

Though she heard every word, she knew she wasn't taking it all in. How could she, when this shaking inside her kept growing, building, threatening to tear her apart? And yet something of his meaning seeped through. He had *always* wanted her. Even that night in the gazebo. She hadn't been the only one.

"But then it changed, didn't it, Nellie?"

She nodded, shutting her eyes. Oh, yes, it had changed. She fought the urge to put her hands on his head, letting them get lost in the thick silk of his hair. That would be a fatal mistake. He had said *want,* not love. For him, those two things were not the same. For her, they were inseparable. But she wanted to touch him. She balled her hands into fists. She wanted to so much.

At first, when he pulled back, she felt no alarm. His voice was still smooth, still husky, and she leaned her head against the tree, exposing her neck in a half-conscious symbol of invitation and acquiescence.

"It changed," he went on, "because somehow you spotted the chink in my armor, didn't you?" A rough emotion seemed to have scraped his voice raw, and her eyes flew open at the sound.

"What?" She drew her chin in protectively and spoke the syllable on a stunned intake of breath.

"How did you know, Nellie? Was it that obvious? I thought I was hiding it so well. But you saw how you could take advantage of it. And that's how we ended up with the disaster in the gazebo, isn't it?"

Disaster? Her eyes searched his face, trying to see past the narrowed eyes, grim mouth and flared nostrils, trying to find something, anything warm or sympathetic. Could he really still think she had engineered that night just to spite him, just to make trouble for him? If it was true that he'd always wanted her, couldn't he understand that the same desire had driven her?

But there was nothing gentle in his face. She put her hands to her chest, seeking to hold back the pain that flowered there. "No, Edan—"

"Yes." He moved even closer. "But do you know what the real disaster is, Nell?"

It was difficult to make her lips work. "What?"

"You're still driving me mad." He ran his hands roughly across her collarbones, from one shoulder to the other, and pressed her back against the tree. The bark dug into her scalp. "I still want you so much I can't see straight."

Spoken in that way, the admission should have brought her little pleasure. Clearly he despised the unwanted desires he couldn't banish. And yet, in spite of everything, a flash of irrational hope went off inside her. He wanted her. For years she'd been sinking in an ocean that seemed bottomless, and miraculously her feet had finally touched the ground.

He wanted her. She swallowed hard. "Edan, can't we forget about that night in the gazebo? It was so long ago. Can't you ever—"

"No, damn it. I can't." She could feel the tension in his hands, hear it in his voice. "At least not when I'm with you like this. It all comes back. Takes my breath away like a sucker punch. One touch, one kiss, and I'm twenty years old again, unable to stop myself." His breathing was forced, and his voice was tight and furious. "I hate it. I hate you for making me feel this helpless, and I hate myself for letting you."

"I understand...." And amazingly she did. Didn't that one sentence sum up the way she had felt all these years? Bewitched, enslaved, and always railing against the sorcery that held her. "I wanted you, too." She steeled herself against the blackness of his eyes. "I never meant to hurt you. I—"

"Shh." This time the sibilant whisper wasn't gentle. It was sharp, with an undertone of desperation. "I don't want to talk about it. I don't want to think about it. I just want—"

He broke off with a curse. Swallowing painfully, she stared at him. He didn't believe her. To him, she was a manipulative schemer who had abused their mutual attraction to further her own ends.

And yet it was clear how much he wanted her. The stiff grip of his fingers, the hard thrust of his body, spoke of the war that raged within him. She didn't try to resist. He had to fight this battle himself.

For the first time since she had returned to Wildings, a curious peace came over her as she realized that she had already, on some unconscious level, fought her own battle. For better or worse, it was decided. She wanted him. Despite what came later, she wanted him one more time.

She didn't ask for forgiveness, didn't require that he understand. Her needs were simpler than they had ever been. She only wanted to touch him. She wanted them to share one heartbeat, one breath, one body, for one transmuting moment. She'd live on that forever.

Now she just had to wait. Though heat simmered in every vein, threatening to bring her blood to a roiling boil, she tried to stay calm.

And when she thought she could no longer breathe, he released her shoulder. His hand slid up, across her cheek and then over her mouth. Her lips parted as his finger pushed between them, demanding the admittance she would have given freely. She shut her eyes as his finger went deeper, and her entire body clenched in reaction.

"I have to have you." His voice was low and desperate. His whole body was pressed against hers, and she could feel how the longing had taken hold of him. His decision was made, too. She could feel it. But he was not at peace with his. "Now."

Yes. She let her lips tell him silently, tightening around his finger, pulling its salty warmth into her mouth. Oh, yes. She didn't let herself think what she would have done if he had decided to walk away. Her blood was screaming for him, and she wanted him with a pain sharper than she could bear. It had been so long.

When he took his hand away, she whimpered, but he smothered the sound with his lips, and in one powerful movement he scooped her up into his arms. Without taking his lips from hers, he carried her further into the stand of oaks, to a place where the sun shot through the thick canopy of leaves with narrow shafts of light, and the air smelled wet and green.

He lowered her onto a patchwork quilt of leaves, his mouth still drinking from hers with a wild and unquenchable thirst. His hands were rough as they reached under her sweater, shoving her bra up and away from the soft roundness of her breasts.

But she didn't mind his roughness. Her hands were rough, too, as they slid over his shirt, seeking, craving and finally finding the heat of his skin underneath.

He groaned into her mouth as she touched him, and rolled toward her, throwing one leg over hers. As his knee moved up, stabbing her with a delicious pain, she felt the full power of his need. And she arched toward it, running her hands down to his hips, urging him closer.

His hands moved, too, sliding under the clasp of her jeans toward the very core of her. As she moaned, writhing beneath his fiery touch, he tore open the button and zipper, and shoved her jeans down around her thighs.

It was happening too fast to stop. His urgency was rising, and she felt her own need surging out of control. She reached for his belt buckle, desperately seeking release from the unbearable aching. She'd regret this later—in some dim recess of her mind she realized that—but for the moment only the pressure inside her was real. If he didn't take her now she would split in two.

With fumbling fingers she managed to loosen his belt, but when she reached for the button of his jeans he stopped her, locking her wrist in a grip as unyielding as a steel handcuff.

"No." She hardly recognized his voice, thick and hoarse and angry. "No. We're not going to do this."

She struggled under him, twisting her hand until his fingers burned the skin of her wrist. She wouldn't let him change his mind. He couldn't mean it. Again she arched against him, shamelessly trying to break his control.

"No." The syllable was a tortured groan, and he pulled away raising himself over her. "Be still."

"Edan . . ." She sounded strange, too, her voice as thick and miserable as her body. "Edan, you have to . . . We have to."

He took deep slow breaths, turning his face from hers, and tension rippled through his arms as he held himself above her.

"Don't leave me." She was frightened by the iron control she saw in him. She couldn't let him go now. Struggling to breathe around the pulsing need that had spread through her body, she whispered, "Don't leave me."

Finally he looked back at her. "Leave you?" He dipped his head to her breast. "Never." Putting his hands beneath her shoulder blades, he lifted her toward him. "Never."

"But you said . . ." She was losing her focus, caught up in the swirling clouds of passion. His mouth was so hot, so soft and firm, gentle and savage, all at once. She began to shiver, and her nipples tightened under his tongue.

He raised his head. His lips were swollen and his dark hair tumbled toward fevered eyes. "I said we're not going to do this, not this way. We're not fumbling teenagers now, Nellie. If I'm going to make love to you, I'm going to do it right. It's going to be slow." Leaning back, he dragged her jeans, inch by inch, from her legs. "It's going to be long." Her white silk panties followed, and she shut her eyes as the shivering mounted deep inside her. "And it's going to be wonderful."

As he had commanded, she lay very still while he knelt in front of her, stroking her legs. His loose belt buckle dangled coldly against her skin, but his fingers teased at the soft inner edges of her thighs with a warmth that turned her muscles to liquid.

Small twitches and involuntary shifts were her only external reaction as his fingers explored her. Even when his mouth joined the search, bringing a wet heat to the places that were already melting, she forced herself to lie, quiescent, giving every sensation her full attention, never writhing away from the torment but letting it take her into a new world of ultimate abandon.

Expertly he brought her to the edge of that world, then held her there, poised over the void for what seemed like forever. Lost in the sensations, she barely registered that his own breath was coming harder and that his shoulders were trembling slightly.

Finally she opened her eyes, searching for him, searching for something to hold on to. She found his head, taking it in her hands and tracing its strength with her fingertips, finding reassurance in the solid reality of it. He looked up and met her eyes, his own blazing under heavy lids.

As if he read her need, he rose quickly. Then he was above her, entering her, joining her on that precipice. Gratefully she wrapped her arms and legs around him, and he began a slow careful rhythm that seemed to recognize how close to falling she was.

Gradually, as she found her balance, the rhythm began to build. Faster, faster, then slower again whenever she began to slip. It seemed to go on that way for hours, though time in that world was not measured by clocks. They held each other desperately, flirting with the fall, until at last she could stand it no longer.

"Now," she cried, or maybe she didn't, but somehow he heard her, and the rhythm went wild. That strange electric world she had just discovered exploded beneath them, and they fell, still locked, into the void, which wasn't a void at all but a shivering world of gushing melting suns and shooting stars.

The void came later.

CHAPTER EIGHT

WITH EYES TIGHTLY SHUT, Eleanor tried to hold reality at bay. Though she'd told herself she could accept whatever came, now that the moment was here she wasn't ready. But it was not to be postponed. Her head cleared; her body steadied. And, as if an anesthetic had suddenly worn off, her heart began to ache.

The dream of a private sensual paradise disappeared, and the sordid real world asserted itself. Looking down at herself, she saw that twigs had scratched her arms, and bits of grass clung to her bare sweaty legs. And—somehow this was the worst—she still had her shirt and shoes on. She felt like the leading lady in a sleazy movie.

She turned her head to one side, away from Edan, who had not spoken. Only now did she realize that she had been praying he would release her from the promise she had made to herself. One word...one small wonderful word would take away the shame and the pain. But he didn't speak.

Her heart swelled until she had to fight off tears. This was all too horribly familiar. She might have been sixteen again. But she couldn't give in to it. She wasn't a naive teenager. She was twenty-five, and she had made love to Edan fully aware of the pain that was to follow. She wouldn't disgrace herself by weeping and whining. Not this time.

No, this time everything would be different. She wouldn't go crawling to him, begging, holding her pathetic love out like a child eagerly sharing a favorite battered toy, only to have him brush it away, as if it was too grubby to touch.

To help her steady her resolve, she let memory present its most painful picture—Edan's hard face when she had sought him out some days after the episode in the gazebo. "Go away, Nell," he had said. "Just go away." Humiliated, she had slunk off to grieve alone.

Her chest tightened. *Never* again.

She heard him righting his clothing, and gathering every ounce of strength she could find, she reached for her own things, whisking the dirt from them with shaking fingers.

"We should be getting back," she said as she slipped them on. The narrow ankle of her jeans caught on her shoe and she yanked harder. "I promised I'd help decorate for the party tonight."

After a small silence, he turned slowly, his whole body stiffening. "What?"

Yanking again at the recalcitrant jeans, she shot him a quick glance. His face was impassive, of course—what had she expected? *He* never gave his emotions away. *He* was never vulnerable, never caught with aching need glistening in his eyes for anyone to see.

Except . . . her traitorous, ever hopeful heart tried to argue. Except . . . moments ago when his eyes had been on fire. Taking one more look at their cool blackness, she shook herself mentally. He had succumbed to physical desire, but fiery eyes and urgent fingers didn't add up to anything but sex. She made herself be tougher, trying to harden herself against the pain of wishful thinking. Lust, Eleanor, is not even a distant cousin to love.

She blinked to clear away the foolish tears. "I said I'd help hang the Japanese lanterns for the dance." Still not sure that her eyes could pass inspection, she tilted her face to the clear bright sky. "I hope it doesn't rain. It won't be the same if we have to move the party inside—"

"For heaven's sake," he broke in violently. "Do you want to talk about the weather right now?"

"Well, the dance *is* the climax of the reunion," she said, deliberately obtuse. No, damn him, she didn't want to talk about the weather. She didn't want to talk about anything at all. She didn't know how these casual interludes were handled. When it came to the language of passion, she was illiterate.

Frustrated, she wrestled with her foot, her hands growing clumsy with impatience. If only she could get these blasted jeans on, she could leave.

"Let me." He reached out and wrapped one hand around her ankle, the other around the toe of her shoe. Looking away, she refused to think about his strong persuasive fingers. "Easy does it," he murmured. Instead of pulling, he coaxed and twisted, and soon the shoe slipped through.

"Thanks." Hopping to her feet, she skimmed the jeans up over her legs and fumbled with the zipper. She tried not to notice him sitting at her feet, his face at thigh level, though her skin tingled as if his breath could pass through the denim. Tucking her shirt into the waistband, she affected an insouciance she scarcely felt and looked around. "I guess Sweetpea has wandered off."

"Nell." He rose smoothly, his body towering over hers, and put his hand behind her neck, under her tousled hair. "We need to talk."

"No." She stepped back, shaking her head firmly. "No, we don't." She was pleased with the sound of her voice. No trembling, no hint of whining or begging. Now he'd see whether she had grown up or not. He'd see that she wasn't any longer the naive girl who thought one chance sexual episode, however pleasant, was a sacred exchange of vows. He'd see that she knew all too well that a man could want, and take, and then forget.

"Look, Edan, just let it go, okay?" She smiled ruefully. At least she hoped it was rueful. It felt wobbly and childish. "I don't really know what happened. Maybe we, well, maybe we both needed to do that. Maybe we were looking for closure and—"

"Don't give me that damn psychobabble, Nell. *Closure?*"

"Well, whatever you want to call it." She tried to sound reasonable. "Anyway, now it's out of our systems, and we can get on with our lives...." Her sensible argument dwindled off, absurd even to her own ears.

He was silent for a long while, and she was acutely conscious of the noises of the day: the clear whistle of a robin, the gurgle of a bluebird, the rustling sweep of the wind through the treetops. They might have been the only humans on earth.

Fidgeting uncomfortably under his searching silence, she leaned down to brush slivers of grass from her tennis shoes. Perspiration trickled down her neck. It was getting hot. She realized that it must be at least midmorning. People would be wondering where they were.

"I guess Sweetpea went home," she said, finally breaking the silence since apparently he wasn't going to. "I'll walk back."

He frowned. "Is that all you have to say?"

She gave him a smile. She was beginning to feel steadier and her smiles felt more convincing. "What were you expecting me to say? Should I deliver some outraged monologue from a Victorian melodrama?" She shook her head. "We're both beyond that, aren't we?"

Now he grinned, too, slowly, and the effect was so unpleasant she wondered uncomfortably whether her own smile had looked that way, all smug and distant and somehow hurtful.

"I was actually expecting something more like 'I'm going to tell my father,'" he said, his grin growing more disagreeable. "Oh, sorry. That should be 'I'm going to tell my grandmother,' shouldn't it?"

She stiffened, trying to shield herself from the barb, but it didn't work. The insult buried itself in her heart, and it stung—horribly. But she forced herself not to show it, raising her chin and speaking with an airy defiance. "That would be a waste of time. Grandmother wouldn't be a bit angry. In fact, she'd be delighted."

"All the more reason to tell her, I'd have thought." He leaned against a tree, looking cool and collected. She had to fight the utterly Victorian urge to slap his face. "The future of Wildings would be assured."

Damn him. She took a couple of deep breaths before she responded, terrified that she might lose her hard-won dignity. How dared he accused her of that?

"Listen, Edan," she said, her voice husky from the effort to keep it level. "*You* may have ulterior motives for what you do, but don't assume everyone is as calculating as you are. This—'' she gestured toward the spot where they had lain ''—happened simply because we wanted to make love. Because it was nice. That's all.''

He looked at the spot, too, a grassy opening between two tall trees. The green blades were still crushed from their weight, and Eleanor had to force away a mental picture of them lying in each other's arms.

''Sorry,'' he said blandly, bringing his eyes back to her with a lazy grin. ''I didn't realize this was an everyday occurrence for you.''

''You know it's not!'' she protested in a rising tone before she realized how blatantly he was baiting her. ''Oh, forget it,'' she said, blushing, and turned away. Her heart was already bruised. She didn't have to stand here and let him take punches at it.

But she didn't get far. In two seconds his hand was on her arm, whisking her around to face him. He was still smiling, but his eyes were blazing.

''Actually, I really thought you might want to say something altogether different. Something like—'' his voice dipped lower ''—something like 'I love you, Edan.'''

He pulled her close, taunting her with the smell and feel of his body. She tried not to breathe. She tried not to feel. But her body had learned the shape of him, and without her approval it was curving toward him. ''Try it,'' he murmured. ''Say 'I love you, Edan.'''

For one moment she was trapped by his eyes, so deep, so gray—fathomless, but with a shadow moving just under the surface, like a predator in the depths of the ocean. She even thought, for that mesmerized moment, that she might say it. Her lips wanted to, as keenly as they wanted to feel his mouth against hers one more time.

But then the weakness passed, and she found the strength she needed.

She pulled herself free and walked away from him, into the clear field under a sun so bright it had forced open the roses and sucked the dew from every petal.

But in her heart there was only midnight and mist.

SWEATPEA WAS STANDING placidly in her stall when Eleanor got back, munching on her lunch with obvious indifference to Eleanor's mood, which, after a long hot trudge in the sun with only her troubled thoughts for company, was decidedly grim.

Eleanor patted the mare wearily as she went by, eager to get into the house and wash the feel of Edan from her skin. She noticed that Shadow was home, too. Naturally the stallion had been waiting obediently for Edan just outside the stand of trees. Was there any living creature who didn't slavishly adore the man?

As the two of them had passed her in the meadow, Edan had offered her a ride with apparent courtesy. She had turned it down with an equally phony courteousness, as he of course had known she would. "It's pretty hot," he'd pointed out helpfully, as though she hadn't noticed the perspiration that gleamed on her face or the way her shirt clung to her torso.

It might have seemed churlish, but she couldn't accept. It had been all she could do to mount Sweetpea earlier; Shadow's massive size and strength were far too intimidating. And besides, riding tandem with Edan, her back against his chest . . . Uh-uh. She'd walk to the moon first.

She hurried out of the stables, keeping her mind steadfastly on her bath to avoid the miserable thoughts that battered her willpower. What insanity had possessed her? Why had she allowed herself to be bedded in the woods, like a lusty teenager or a ten-dollar—

No, she simply wouldn't think about it.

But it was easy to see why he despised her. It undoubtedly fed his ego to think she couldn't resist him, to think she had never managed to outgrow her pathetic puppy love. And a gratified ego didn't necessarily lead to respect. Clearly he figured she was—

No, she'd take a shower instead of a bath. It was quicker, a more violent cleansing.

But, why, oh why, had she done it? Had she really been stupid enough to believe one more memory would make it easier to live without him? She kicked a small rock out of her path. Of course not. That had just been the desperate rationalization her aching body had offered her reluctant mind. What a fool she was! After five years of hard work and pain, she had finally begun to reclaim her soul, and now she had handed it back—

No, a bath, then a day of hard work, and tomorrow they'd all leave.

Suddenly, through her tumultuous mental struggle, she heard a whimper. She stopped and listened carefully, shutting out her inner chaos. She frowned. The sound was too soft to be one of the horses. And it certainly wasn't a cat. The noise came again, low and miserable, and struck a chord in her memory. It sounded like a little girl.

Following the sound, she entered the barn that adjoined the stables. Lit only by the dusty ribbons of sunlight that had found the cracks between the planks, the building had clearly fallen into some disrepair in the past few years. It still smelled of hay and leather, though, and she remembered how she had loved to come here, to climb to the loft to hide from everyone, Edan in particular.

With the memory came a flash of insight. The child she could hear now must be Kelly. Poor kid. Something terrible must have happened.

Eleanor hesitated only briefly, wondering whether she could possibly help the girl when she felt so unhappy and mixed-up herself, but she shoved the doubts aside and placed her foot on the ladder. It was the same advice she would have given any of her kids at the center—if you want to forget your problems, concentrate on somebody else's.

When she reached the top of the ladder, she knew her instincts had been right. Over in the corner, where even the feeble rays of light couldn't reach, Kelly Ridgeway was huddled, her head on her knees and her arms wrapped tightly around her shins, the picture of misery. Eleanor hoisted herself onto the loft floor and went over to sit down beside the other girl.

"I used to come here a lot," she said after giving Kelly a minute to adjust to the idea of her presence. "I always felt a million miles away from my problems up here."

"Yeah?" Kelly said to her knees. "What kind of problems did *you* have?"

Eleanor had to smile at Kelly's tone, which suggested a profound skepticism as to whether Eleanor's problems could have amounted to much. The young were so self-absorbed, so sure that they were pioneering new emotional territory with each heartache.

"Nothing very original," Eleanor said, sitting cross-legged and leaning her back against the rough wall. "My parents got divorced, then they both got remarried to people who already had kids, and it didn't seem like anybody really wanted me around."

Kelly looked up, forgetting for the moment to cry. Her face was dirty, tracked with lines of tears and dust, and her eyes were red. "What'd you do?"

Eleanor sorted through the memories, trying to find an honest answer. "I think I pretty much just pouted for about five years." She opened her eyes and looked sheepishly at Kelly. "I was really mad."

"Jeez." Kelly grimaced. "Five years! Didn't you get sick of it? I mean, I'm really tired of being depressed all the time. It's no fun."

Eleanor smiled again. Edan had been right. With such a healthy attitude, Kelly was going to be fine. "Eventually I did," she admitted. "But I wish I'd gotten sick of it sooner. I wasted a lot of time being miserable."

Kelly nodded in emphatic agreement. "I know. That's what I keep telling my mother and father. Get along or get divorced, for Pete's sake. Just stop all this yelling and screaming."

"Wouldn't it be nice if it was that easy?" Eleanor sighed. "Actually it's a good sign that they're fighting. It means they don't want to give up. It means they still care enough about each other to bother."

Something in that little homily rang a bell inside her. She'd recognized long ago that if she hadn't cared deeply for Edan she wouldn't have been angry with him. So, might the converse be true? If *he* didn't care about *her* . . .

She shook the thought away, unnerved by the way her heart kept trying to hang on, kept trying to explain his tempers and his insults. Besides, she'd come up into the loft to sort out Kelly's problems, not her own.

"Yeah, well, it's sure a pain in the neck to live with," Kelly grumbled, blowing gently into a shaft of sunlight to watch the dust motes dance. "Sometimes I wish Carmela and I could go off and live by ourselves."

"Who's Carmela?" A favorite aunt, perhaps, or a special friend? That might account for Kelly's practicality. Kids who had a network of outside supporters usually coped better with family crises.

"She's our housekeeper," Kelly said, but hastened to elaborate, as though afraid that Eleanor might underrate the marvelous Carmela. "But that's just what we call her. She's cool, really fun and pretty. She's been with us since I was a baby. She's like a second mom."

Then Kelly frowned. "Actually, Carmela's more like a *first* mom. She's a heck of a lot more interested in what I'm doing and how I'm feeling than my real mom is."

With effort, Eleanor bit back the urge to defend Kelly's mother. It wouldn't do any good, and besides, Kelly might be right. Not every mother was born with fully developed maternal instincts.

"You're lucky to have Carmela," Eleanor said, meaning it. What would she have done without Gran all those years? Everybody needed to feel important to *someone*. "In fact, you're kind of lucky to have two moms."

"Yeah, I guess so." But the response was perfunctory. Kelly stood up, obviously feeling recovered enough to be impatient with the conversation, and brushed briskly at the seat of her jeans. "It's hot up here," she said with annoyed surprise, as though noticing the fact for the first time.

"I know," Eleanor said, lifting her own hair and dabbing at her damp neck. "I always tried to schedule my emotional traumas in the winter."

"Good thinking," Kelly said with a grin, picking a cobweb out of her hair and wiping dust from her face with the back of her hand. "This is really gross."

Eleanor smiled a lopsided smile. If only she had been that resilient at fifteen. Or at twenty-five. She stood up, too, though she was suddenly reluctant to leave the quiet isolation of the loft, however hot and grimy it was. She stared out the grain window. Somewhere down there in the real world, her own problems were waiting, all six feet two inches of them. Better to stay up here.

Avoidance, she heard Frank saying. *That's right,* she answered him mentally. *Like you'd avoid sticking your hand in a fire.*

But Kelly was already on her way down the ladder, humming an off-key rendition of a popular rock song. Eleanor decided that maybe they should switch places next time, and she'd let Kelly be the counselor.

"Hey, I've got to hang some paper lanterns," she called down to Kelly as she began to make her own way to the ground. "Want to help?"

Kelly looked up, a sassy smile on her face. "Wow," she said with lighthearted sarcasm. "What a thrill."

But Eleanor could tell the offer pleased her, and in spite of everything, she finished descending the ladder feeling considerably better than she had when she'd ascended it.

BY TWILIGHT everything was ready. The band was tuning up in the gazebo, the wisteria was perfuming the air and the Japanese lanterns glowed warmly against the purple sky.

People had already started to arrive, clustering around the enormous crystal punch bowl—where circles of fruit floated on a sweet liquid sea—and plucking strawberries from the huge red pyramids on either side. Uniformed waiters moved quietly among the guests, handing out long-stemmed champagne glasses and artistic hors d'oeuvres.

It was a pretty picture—Wildings at its best. Only the immediate family knew that the nicked lip of the punch bowl was turned to the back or that the champagne glasses were rented, the hors d'oeuvres homemade. The champagne was first-rate, though. Charlotte had insisted on that. Eleanor and Kelly exchanged smiles over the success of their efforts and hurried up to the house to dress.

By the time Eleanor had buttoned herself into her gown, she knew she'd be the last one down. She left her hair loose, haste weighing in more heavily than vanity, and pinched teardrop pearl earrings onto her earlobes, hoping they would supply enough glamour to make up the difference.

As she hurried into the hallway, she passed Gina's room. Surprised to see the lights still on, she stuck her head into the doorway. "Coming, Gina?"

Eleanor had to clamp her mouth shut to keep from gasping. Gina stood facing the door, her head bent, her long brown hair lifted to bare her back. Edan was behind her, handsome in his immaculate tuxedo, frowning over the snaps at the back of Gina's dress.

Not that there was much of a back to it. Eleanor knew full well that Gina could have handled those snaps. They weren't much more than waist-high. Why, just moments ago Eleanor had been struggling with the long row of small pearl buttons on her own dress. And no one had heard *her* asking for help....

Edan looked at her but didn't speak, apparently deciding to let Gina explain. Their eyes met over Gina's lowered head and slowly, with a silent insolence, Edan drew one brow up to an arched question. Clearly he found the situation amusing.

"Later, Eleanor," Gina said, her voice muffled. "Tell Charlotte I'll be there in a jiffy, would you, honey?"

It was clearly an invitation to leave. Edan heard it, and his mouth quirked into a small smile. What the hell was so funny about it? Like the storybook child trying to plug the hole in the dike, Eleanor tried to stop the flood of irritation that threatened to overwhelm her. What difference did it make if Gina used such obvious flirtatious ploys?

And what difference did it make if Edan was fool enough to fall for them? What difference did it make, really, if he buttoned or unbuttoned the dress of every woman at the party?

But it did matter. A tingling anger centered at the small of her back stiffened her, and she felt paralyzed in the doorway. It made no sense, but she absolutely hated the sight of Edan's dark hands on Gina's pale back. And she hated leaving them there together.

But even worse, she hated that he knew all these things, that he could read her face as if it were written in his own private language. Immobilized by his quizzical unshrinking expression, Eleanor had to force herself to turn away, had to pry her hand off the doorknob.

"Okay," she managed, ashamed of the surly note that had crept into her voice. "I'll see you downstairs, then."

Slamming the door behind her, she fairly flew down the stairs and out onto the back veranda. Pausing at the balustrade to catch her breath, she surveyed the guests. A good number of neighbors and townsfolk had been invited, and Eleanor wondered if there were any men her age. Handsome, broad-shouldered young men who would whirl her around and flirt shamelessly with her, admiring her pretty yellow dress and her big blue eyes...

When Edan came down—*if* he came down—she was darn well going to be dancing. Let him catch her eye with that laughing arrogance then.

CHAPTER NINE

HER HEART SANK as she spied Allen Ridgeway weaving through the crowd in her direction. As determined as she was to be dancing when Edan arrived, she drew the line there. Allen Ridgeway needed to dance with his wife, and Eleanor was feeling testy enough to tell him that if he dared to bother her.

But luck intervened. From the other side of the porch, a blond young man found his courage just in time and came up to invite her to dance.

Though she didn't know him, she accepted with relief. Leaving Allen stranded halfway to the porch, she gave the young man a smile dazzling enough to make him trip slightly as they descended the steps. She must have overdone it, because as she moved into his arms his hands were subtly shaking. He was, she noticed, very young and very good-looking, but she couldn't help comparing his hesitant manner with Edan's rough confidence.

But that was unfair, and she thrust the thought away. Though her partner's conversation was only the most predictable party talk—how good the band was, how nice the weather, how lovely her dress—she kept smiling into his handsome face as if she found his comments the height of clever repartee.

The minutes dragged on. Eventually she exchanged the young man for a new partner, one handsome face for another, and then another, until her jaw ached from the effort of holding that huge vapid grin in place. She fought back a sigh of boredom. Had men always been this dull? But of course the men were not to blame. She glared at the veranda, at the stubbornly closed doors. Wasn't Edan *ever* going to come down?

Though it seemed she hadn't taken her eyes from the door for a single second, she must have. All of a sudden Edan was cutting in, dismissing her partner with polite apology and gathering her into his arms as if she belonged there.

Her smile froze as his hands wrapped around her waist, pulling her toward him. She was torn between a foolish relief that he was no longer upstairs with Gina and irritation at his presumptuous takeover. The warring emotions created a standoff, and for a moment she couldn't speak at all.

"That's a high-wattage smile, Nellie," he said, a low ripple of mischief in his voice. "I wouldn't have thought Mitchell was entertaining enough to warrant it."

Surprised, she eased the corners of her mouth into a more natural curve. "Mitchell?" she asked, at a loss.

"Brad Mitchell." Edan inclined his head toward the gazebo, where the thin young man he had supplanted stood, leaning sulkily against the lattice and watching them with an expression of intense gloom. "Your departed swain, who apparently would like to toss me into the Mississippi."

"Oh, yes." She frowned. She didn't care for Edan's sarcastic tone. "Yes. He was delightful. He had such funny stories."

"Really?" Edan smiled, one eyebrow high. "Life in the funeral-parlor business must be more amusing than I'd imagined."

Oh, good grief, was Mitchell the one who was a mortician? She blushed, realizing she had completely forgotten every word Brad Mitchell had uttered. Meeting Edan's eyes, she saw the laughter lurking there. And she couldn't help it. She laughed, too.

"Well, perhaps I was thinking of someone else," she said, trying to smother her laughter.

"Undoubtedly."

His tone was smug, and she knew immediately what he meant. He must have seen her watching the door and automatically assumed she was looking for him. What arrogance! She pressed her lips together. The fact that he was right only increased her irritation.

For an instant she considered leaving, just wriggling out of his embrace and stalking away. But as soon as she tensed her muscles for flight, he tightened his grip, making escape difficult without attracting attention. Frustrated, she looked around them at the other couples dancing under the lanterns, the children chasing each other around the oaks, the older folks clustered around the tables of food, arguing happily. She even saw Charlotte, festive in blue silk, watching contentedly from her lawn-chair throne.

Charlotte caught her eye and smiled. And Eleanor, smiling back, relaxed into Edan's arms again. She couldn't spoil this night for Charlotte. No matter how annoying Edan Bond was.

Instead, she'd annoy him back.

"Yes, it must have been someone else. Derek, perhaps?" She bit her lower lip, pretending to consider. "Yes, I think it was Derek. I've danced with him several times. A very special man—do you know him?"

"No." Edan wasn't laughing anymore. His voice deepened and his hands tightened, pressing her body harder into his. "I'm afraid not."

"Oh, then you should meet him," she said brightly, and though she was a bit ashamed of herself she couldn't help being pleased with his reaction. His ego needed taking down a peg. "He's quite charming. A doctor, I think, from Baton Rouge, and he's here with his sister, who's married to a Wilding." She scanned the crowd. "Perhaps I can find him and introduce you—"

"Shut up, Nellie." Edan didn't even pretend to be interested in the charming Derek, which was fortunate, considering there was no such person. Uncomfortably aware that she was being childish but satisfied that she had made her point, Eleanor subsided.

After a moment, Kelly Ridgeway danced past them, looking animated and quite lovely in a simple red dress. Her partner seemed enchanted. Eleanor winked at Kelly as she swept past.

"Kelly seems happy," Edan said, watching the girl. "Your talks must be doing her a lot of good."

Eleanor shook her head. "I haven't done much of anything, really. Kelly doesn't need my help, not on a professional level. All things considered, she's extremely well adjusted."

"And you're extremely modest." Edan offered the compliment in a matter-of-fact way. "Remember how Kelly was when she arrived? Mad at the world. As if you couldn't have paid her to smile. Now look at her."

Glad of an excuse to turn her head away, Eleanor tried not to be excessively pleased. But Edan so rarely said anything good about her, and it felt terrific. "She's a great kid," she said, avoiding a direct response.

"And apparently you're a great counselor. That center is lucky to have you."

After that, his pulling her closer seemed amazingly natural. She relaxed, letting her head rest against his shoulder, which seemed to have been designed just for her.

She shouldn't have. She should have kept chattering idiotically. She should have asked him to go get her a plate of strawberries. She should have grabbed a passing champagne glass and gulped down some liquid courage. She should have done anything except what she did—shut her eyes and give herself over to the dance.

Neither of them spoke for a long time, and in the unguarded silence she didn't notice herself growing more and more aware of him, aware of his scent, aware of the way their bodies touched and parted as they swayed to the music.

Suddenly her eyes flew open, all her senses tingling with the awareness. As if he knew it, Edan lessened their movement until it was only a subtle sway that was more an embrace than a dance, and their bodies settled into each other, lines following lines, swells meeting hollows, like the mist settling over the river.

When finally they were perfectly matched, when they met at every point, he began to move his hands.

At first it was only a gentle massage, a kneading at the small of her back that tightened rather than relaxed her muscles. A relentless pressure built under his hands, somewhere between her hipbones, and she shifted, trying to ease it.

But the movement was ill-advised. As she tried to writhe free, his hands slipped down, his fingers resting just above the subtle slope of her buttocks. And then he pressed.

She inhaled sharply and closed her eyes. In reflex her pelvis moved up, just a fraction of an inch, but it was a sign that her body was seeking the part of his that would ease the pain, the key that would unlock her and release the pressure.

But her gown, his clothes, were in the way. Blindly her hands left his shoulders and found the small of his back, resting there with a delicate pressure, a faint restrained echo of his touch. It was an admission, and he understood it. His hands dropped and spread, the heat from his fingers burning through her skirt as though the soft silk was no barrier at all.

Her breath came quickly, and his was deep and hot against her ear. They were barely moving, lost in the music, lost in each other.

Then, cruelly, the music stopped. The applause around them was like scattered gunfire, startling them back to reality. With an almost inaudible cry, she dropped her hands from his back and pulled herself erect.

For a moment she simply stared, the haze of sensuality clouding her vision. She fought to get her breathing under control. When she could see him clearly again, she saw that he was smiling, a cold mirthless smile.

"It's a good thing we've got all that out of our systems, isn't it?" he said sarcastically, throwing her own words, spoken only this morning with such false bravado, back at her. "Otherwise this could get rather out of hand."

After that she couldn't bring herself to dance with anyone else. She sat next to Charlotte for a long time, greeting the cousins and neighbors she hadn't seen for years and watching Edan out of the corner of her eye.

Obviously he had no lingering aversion to dancing. As she watched, he partnered every woman in the place, even Kelly, who chattered happily through the entire song. He played the host perfectly, sharing his attentions equally with the youngest and the oldest, the plainest and the prettiest. The only woman he danced with more than once was Gina, whose fondness for Edan was surpassed apparently only by her fondness for champagne. Tonight she was indulging both passions freely.

As they spun by her for the third time, Gina's arms wrapped around Edan's neck and her beaming face tilted toward his, Eleanor stood up abruptly. Excusing herself to her grandmother, she wandered away from the crowd down toward the river. The grass grew sparsely there, and she had to lift her skirt to keep the yellow silk from dragging through the dirt.

She needed to be alone. The night was full of the sweet smell of wisteria and the sad cry of violins; her heart was full of confusion and a loneliness that a hundred distant cousins could never take away.

At the edge of the bluff she stopped, listening to the slow roll of the river as though it would tell her the answer to all her questions, if only she could decode its message. She sat gingerly on the edge of a rock, her skirt bunched in her hand.

What was she going to do? How was she going to live with this new crack in her heart? She couldn't see Edan without aching. She couldn't touch him without melting. She couldn't even think of him without pain. What was she going to do?

Raising her face to the sky, she tried to make her mind a blank, but the wind tugged lightly at the ends of her hair, tickling it against her bare back as if to nudge her toward a decision.

Tomorrow the reunion was officially over and all the Wildings would scatter again, back to their homes, their jobs, their families and friends.

She was supposed to leave, too. Upstairs in her suitcase a ticket to California lay waiting, ready to take her away from the confusion and the whole miserable battle over Wildings.

She knew now that she would probably lose that battle.

She had seen the love and trust in Charlotte's eyes as she watched Edan, heard the happiness in her voice when she talked to him. And she had to admit that Edan's devotion appeared to be genuine. After all, as he was so fond of pointing out, *he* wasn't the one who had spent five years in self-imposed exile. He had been here, mending the porch, reading *War and Peace,* calling the doctor and, in a thousand little ways, being the grandchild Charlotte needed.

Her heart contracted under a powerful assault of shame and regret. She hadn't meant to be selfish. She had truly believed she had to get away. Suddenly she felt like Dorothy in the *Wizard of Oz.* She had run far away to find herself, never realizing that everything she needed was there in her own backyard.

But where were her ruby slippers? Now that she finally understood, she was about to lose the right to stand here and watch the river lumbering by, to gather violets in the spring, to sit in the gazebo and remember . . .

She couldn't stand it. The sense of loss tore at her, and she had the urge to flee, to grab her suitcase this very moment and run a million miles from Wildings, from Edan, from all the things she couldn't bear to lose.

But she didn't move. Bowing her head, she let the pain wash through her, like a storm through the old oaks. And when it passed, she was still there, still strong enough to carry on.

Shutting her eyes, she wrapped her arms around herself and breathed deeply, savoring the particularly Southern smells of voluptuous flowers, loamy woods and the muddy Mississippi. So different from California's hot bright mix of salt air and suntan lotion.

In that moment, filled with the dark fragrant Wildings air, she knew she couldn't bear to leave. Not yet. At least for today, Wildings was still her home. She needed Wildings, and she needed her grandmother. She needed to make peace with her past. Then, if Edan did inherit Wildings, it wouldn't matter as much.

Yes. She opened her eyes. She would stay, even though staying meant constant contact with Edan. But she would find the strength to face that, too. She would stay as long as Charlotte wanted her.

Suddenly she felt lighter, more relaxed than she had since she'd arrived. She would call Frank first thing in the morning and tell him. And she might start looking for a job down here—

"Champagne, Eleanor?"

She whirled at the sound of a male voice, her heart dropping a beat. But it wasn't Edan. It was Brad Mitchell, the young mortician whose dance Edan had interrupted. Her reaction was equal measures of disappointment and relief.

She managed a smile, her conscience pricking her as she remembered her earlier laughter at Brad's expense. "Thanks," she said, reaching for the proffered glass. She glanced back at the water. "The river's beautiful tonight, isn't it? I couldn't resist coming down for a better look."

"Yeah." Brad stepped closer to the edge of the bluff and peered down. "This is definitely a prime piece of property."

The total absence of any romance in his words didn't surprise her. Brad had been the most mundane conversationalist she had encountered tonight. She sipped her champagne and murmured a syllable that sounded agreeable, wondering why he had followed her down here.

"What's Bond going to do with it, do you know?" Brad's face was speculative as he swept his gaze over the grounds. "Turn it into a hotel?"

Frowning, she lowered her glass. She hadn't thought Brad could surprise her, but he had. "Hotel? Why would he do that?"

He laughed. "Same reason anybody would, I guess. Profit. People love anything antebellum. They'll pay big money for that Civil War and mint julep stuff."

Eleanor stiffened, her fingers tightening around the champagne glass, but she tried to smile naturally. "I'd be very surprised if the idea has ever crossed Edan's mind."

Brad tilted his head, apparently considering. "Well, maybe not, but if he's not going to turn it into a hotel, why did he ask the zoning board to allow this property to go commercial?"

"He didn't!" The words came out vehemently, but as soon as she said them she knew how stupid they were.

She didn't have the faintest idea what Edan might have done. She hadn't been here in five years.

"He did, too," Brad contradicted huffily. "I'm on the city council—that's just a sideline in a little city like this, you know—and we okayed his request last winter. He can make a hotel out of this place any time he wants. He's done it with some property up at Natchez already. Couple of places over at Vicksburg, too, I believe."

At first she was too stunned to speak. Her father's company had never been involved in such things before. Wildings Realty had been solely in the business of brokering other people's properties. When had Edan decided to operate hotels?

And what about Charlotte's disdainful criticism of "Rebel Yell Hotels"? Could she know Edan was involved in such things? Would even Charlotte's adoration survive news like that? No, Eleanor thought grimly. She'd be willing to bet Edan had told her grandmother nothing about it.

When Brad began to look at her curiously, she rallied and found her voice. "Hotels? Are you sure?"

"Of course I'm sure. We looked into it before we voted on the zoning. We had to make sure he wouldn't put up something junky. And I have to say the other hotels he's put together are top-notch. Real nice places. Haven't you ever seen them?"

The hand holding her champagne glass began to tremble, and she took another sip to cover the weakness. Obviously Brad thought she knew. And she *should* have known. In all fairness, though, she couldn't blame her ignorance on Edan. She had made it quite clear she wanted nothing to do with her father's business.

But, oh, how Charlotte would hate it if Edan turned their beloved Wildings into a campy taste-of-the-Old

South hotel! She shuddered and took another swallow. She had to talk to Edan. Maybe Brad was wrong. He was rather a pompous sort; he probably enjoyed pretending he knew everything.

Draining her drink in one swallow, she gave him a cool smile.

"Well, I'd better be getting back. My grandmother will be wondering where I am."

He walked with her, and as they neared the party, which was still in full swing, she scanned the crowd for Edan. Finally she spotted him dancing with Monica Ridgeway and clearly charming her socks off. Gina was standing nearby, watching and impatiently awaiting her turn. The champagne was playing havoc, Eleanor realized, with Gina's usual facade of lazy indifference.

Eleanor sighed, plopping her empty glass on a passing tray. As usual, he was knee-deep in women. How on earth was she going to talk to him alone?

SHE DIDN'T.

Hours later, when the dance was over, Eleanor draped her gown across its hanger and sighed with remembered frustration.

A tipsy Gina was a force to be reckoned with. She'd hardly left Edan's side for a single moment. She might as well have been tethered to him by an invisible leash.

On those rare occasions when Gina had managed to pry herself loose, some other young woman had popped up to take her place. Eleanor's efforts to talk to him had been utterly futile. Sighing again, she tugged a long T-shirt over her head and went into the bathroom to remove her makeup.

In the bathroom mirror she saw herself blush as she remembered dancing with Edan. She could almost feel his fingers on her hips. It hadn't taken much, had it? A couple of strategically placed nudges, a little music, and she was putty in his hands. She didn't even have champagne as an excuse.

Out of her system? Hardly. No wonder he had been sarcastic. He knew that, underneath, she wasn't very different from Gina or any of the other flirting, smiling women who had responded so viscerally to his masculinity.

Suddenly angry, she scrubbed hard at the blush with a square of lotion-soaked cotton, scowling at the doe-eyed ninny who stared back at her. She was going to have to be tougher than this if she intended to stay at Wildings.

She was going to have to be tough, too, if she intended to handle the issue Brad Mitchell had brought up. Slipping on a pair of cutoffs and some sandals, she decided to see if Edan was still downstairs. It had been very late when the musicians packed up and the last guest went home, but Edan had stayed to pay the hired help and lock up while Eleanor had taken an exhausted Charlotte to bed.

If he was awake, maybe she could finally talk to him alone. There must be some explanation for the zoning mystery—some explanation that would acquit Edan. She couldn't believe that he was going behind Charlotte's back, making plans to destroy Wildings as soon as he could get his hands on it.

She tried to examine her feelings logically. As furious as she had often been with Edan, she had never thought he was sneaky. He didn't need to be. He had always come straight out and asked for what he wanted, knowing that he was bright enough, talented enough, *adored* enough, to get it. No one had ever been able to say no to him. Not even her.

So why would he suddenly stoop to subterfuge? She eased her door shut behind her, hoping not to awaken Charlotte or Gina, and walked softly down the hall toward his room. She had to see him, had to ask him. If the seeing was more important than the asking, she didn't allow herself to think about it.

A quick glance over the banister showed only blackness, so she tapped on his door. She hesitated a moment, listening to the silence. No response. Where was he? Still outside, perhaps? Maybe he was checking to see that the Japanese lanterns were all safely extinguished.

She went to the window at the end of the hall and looked out. The mist was coming in fast, in swirling streams, as though it had been waiting impatiently for the humans to be gone and could wait no longer. The scattered lawn chairs, opened and empty, seemed sadly abandoned in that eerie landscape. The lanterns hung pale and lifeless. There was no sign of Edan.

A low moan from the door nearest the window startled her, and the brief flash of terror that streaked through her was proof that the ghost stories of her childhood had left their mark. But it was no ghost. It was Gina's room, and it was Gina moaning.

Foolishly Eleanor moved toward the door, ready to offer her help. But almost immediately she heard another noise, the gentle almost hypnotic tones of Edan's voice.

Eleanor's hand froze just before it touched the doorknob and her blood ran cold, mercifully numbing her to the implications of the sounds she heard. Edan and Gina—and the primitive sounds of intimacy. Her frozen hand began to shake, and she let it fall to her side as she edged away from the door.

Like an automaton, she walked backward, her eyes on the door, until she felt the telephone table touch her spine. The contact rattled the phone in its cradle slightly, but not, she thought thankfully, loudly enough to rouse the two behind the door. She groped with her fingertips until she felt the edge of the table and, balancing herself, wheeled and headed for the stairs.

Somehow she reached the kitchen, far enough away from the others to know that she couldn't be heard. Once there, the fragile coating of ice that had been protecting her began to break up, and a river of pain rose in great engulfing waves to replace it.

There was no stopping her tears. As she dropped onto a chair and lay her head on her hands on the kitchen table, they flooded from her, dousing her in heartache.

The echoes of his deep, soothing voice roared in her ears. She knew that voice. She knew, though she didn't want to know, exactly what he was doing right now. She knew where his hands were, how strong they were. She knew what his eyes looked like, what his body felt like. She knew—heaven help her—what Gina was feeling....

It was unbearable. Her body still burned from his touch, still felt raw and swollen where he had loved her. If she shut her eyes, she could still smell his fragrance. She pressed her wet hands to either side of her head, as if she could squeeze the memories out, and her tears fell straight onto the table. She couldn't stand this.

But she had no choice, and gradually the flood abated. Her tears slid slowly down her cheeks, the raging waters receding, and she breathed raggedly, catching on every inhale, shaking on every exhale.

She felt damaged, diminished, like the sagging wisteria after a storm. It had always saddened her, the naked stems left on the vine, the fragile blossoms wrenched out and flung upon the ground, lying with petals limp and darkly bruised, drowning in muddy puddles.

She hated to think of herself that way, and self-respect finally lifted its bowed head. She *wouldn't* be reduced to anything so pitiful.

Taking deep steadying breaths, she struggled to salvage some remnant of pride. This shouldn't have been such a shock. She had known their lovemaking this morning meant nothing permanent. Hadn't she? Could she really have been fooling herself still, dreaming that he would want her again, come to her again?

Well, if she had been, she certainly knew better now. And there was one point she could be proud of: at least he didn't know. She had never let him see how much he mattered to her. She blinked away the last of the tears and lay her head on her folded arms, repeating the words like a soothing mantra. He didn't know. And he never would.

She must have slept there at the table, for, some time later, when the mist had the silvery glow of impending dawn, she awakened to a strange noise. Rubbing her eyes, which were gritty and swollen, she stared out the bay window, confused, barely remembering where she was or why.

At first, still half asleep, she registered nothing of what she saw, her vision blurred and turned inward.

Gradually, though, she began to come out of the sleep-fogged trance. Just outside the window the mist was so thick she could hardly see the yard. And it seemed to be alive, a boiling, thick gray cloud that swirled and pressed against the window.

She frowned, her mind finally working well enough to sense the incongruity. Why was it moving so violently? Above the mist she could see the treetops, and they weren't blowing at all. As she watched, the back of her neck prickled and her heart began to drum at an accelerated tempo. Something was wrong.

After a few endless seconds the mist parted, and she saw the figure of a man. Only an outline. Tall, erect, with military bearing...

Shoving the chair back without concern for the noise, she scrambled to her feet. Who was it? It was too early for anyone to be awake. She couldn't see his face, but his lean body, clad in misty gray, seemed familiar....

But that was ridiculous. She didn't believe in ghosts anymore. She swallowed hard. She didn't. So who was out there? Edan, perhaps?

Slowly the figure moved away, and without stopping to consider the wisdom of her decision to follow, she rushed toward the kitchen door. As she pulled it open, the mist curled in around her feet, and she felt a fleeting moment of uncertainty. She shouldn't go out there all alone. Suppose it was a stranger, an intruder...?

But she couldn't believe that. Something about the man had been too familiar. One of the cousins, perhaps, come back early to give the treasure hunt a last try? Or Edan—would he have left Gina's room so early, perhaps to avoid detection? She had to know.

Once she was outside, the sense of approaching daylight was stronger, and the mist didn't seem as thick. She could vaguely see the man moving across the grounds, at least a hundred yards ahead of her. She followed, her pulse pounding in her ears.

To her surprise, he didn't turn toward the gazebo, and she realized how much she had taken his destination for granted. Whoever it was, Edan or a treasure-hunting cousin, she had expected him to go to the gazebo.

But without hesitation the man turned the opposite way, toward the old slave quarters. Her curiosity intensified, and the beating of her heart slowed. Somehow that made him seem more human. Never in a hundred years had Captain Wilding been sighted at the slave quarters.

In Civil War days, the slave quarters would have been teeming with activity, hardly the place to conduct a secret love affair or to hide anything of value. Besides, Celia Galsworthy had died down by the gazebo, and everyone had always assumed that she had buried her treasure there, so it seemed a natural haunting ground.

In her haste, Eleanor stumbled over a root and, righting herself against a tree trunk, lost sight of the figure in the mist. Damn! But ahead of her loomed the dark rectangle of the last surviving slave cabin. There was no question that this had been his destination.

He must be inside. Suddenly the folly of her actions was apparent to her. It was barely dawn, and she was alone, shrouded by mist, following an unknown man to a deserted cabin. Paralyzed by an attack of nerves, she leaned against the tree and stared at the cabin, as though she could, if she stared hard enough, see through the wooden walls.

She couldn't tell how long she stood there, but the sun climbed doggedly into the sky and the mist began to evaporate. Little by little the outlines of the trees, the azaleas, even the cabin, grew clearer, and her courage returned. No self-respecting robber would bother with an old slave cabin, so it must have been a cousin. She had no reason to be afraid of her cousins.

Still, she approached the cabin cautiously.

"Hello?" The sound was thin. "Anybody there?"

The only answer was silence. When she was close enough, she peered through the window, a foolish fluttering in her stomach betraying the fact that, in spite of the daylight, she still was nervous.

But there was nothing in there. No one. Just the sad bare walls and the undisturbed dust. The only footprints in this cabin were her own and Kelly's, left from the day they had halfheartedly hunted for the treasure here.

How silly that had been! And how obvious—Edan, flirting and hunting with Gina, must have easily guessed why she was avoiding the others. No one ever searched around the slave cabin. It was ridiculous. Why would a gently bred Southern belle like Celia Galsworthy trust her slaves with a secret she couldn't tell her own family? Even the most beloved nanny wouldn't—

Eleanor suddenly again heard Kelly speaking of her housekeeper. *Actually, Carmela's more like a first mom. She's a heck of a lot more interested in what I'm doing and how I'm feeling than my real mom is.*

Eleanor stood very still, staring into the empty cabin. Had poor Celia Galsworthy had a Carmela? Had she had a servant whose love was greater than that of her family, one whose loyalty she could trust with her desperate secret? The small seed of hope suddenly burst into rampant bloom, and Eleanor scrambled up the steps. It was possible. Just barely possible...

With excitement so intense it nearly took her breath away, she began to hunt. Mindless of the splinters, she ran her hands over the rough walls, seeking with her fingers for any unusual grooves, any ill-matched boards. Nothing. She knelt, feeling the floorboards. Dust billowed, choking her, but she continued.

And finally her grimy frantic fingers found it. A thumb-shaped groove that, when pulled, lifted up one narrow floorboard. And just under the board, nestled in a small crude hole, was a box. A dull metal ammunition box. With trembling fingers, she scraped dirt from the lid.

And there, beneath the decades of decay, were the initials and the date, elaborately scrolled on the lid. J.W., 1860.

She had found the treasure.

CHAPTER TEN

FOR THE STAR of a century-old legend, the focus of a hundred years of greed and dreams, the box was ludicrously small.

Eleanor sank back on her heels and stared at it, unable to believe what she was seeing. Placing it across her thighs, she ran her fingers reverently over the filigreed monogram. A shaft of sunlight slanting in through the cabin door touched the box, spotlighting it, as if trying to bring out the latent shine in the long-neglected metal.

So small. And so light. Its weight on her legs was barely noticeable. That, somehow, was the strangest part.

For the first time, she turned her attention to what might be *in* the box. In her bemused rapture, the astonishing fact that there had actually *been* a treasure, and that she had found it, had been more important than determining its value.

Now she faced the possibility that the box might even be empty. She shook it gently, but heard nothing. No clink of gold coins, no clatter of diamonds. And after all, it hadn't exactly been buried ten feet deep. It might be just as Kelly had warned. Some long-gone Wilding might well have found it, spent it and left the empty box behind.

She tried to wedge her fingernails into the rusty ridge that connected top and bottom. But the fit was too tight; one fingernail broke off completely and several others bent painfully back. Sighing, she studied the box, which seemed absolutely airtight, as she absently picked grains of rust from under her nails.

Though it was frustrating, it made sense. Of course an ammunition box would require a tight seal to protect the gunpowder from nasty Southern summer rains. As a treasure chest, it had been a good choice. If anything was left in this box, it would be well-preserved.

She tried again, using the pads of her fingers. She thought she felt the lid give slightly, but it must have been wishful thinking. Inspecting the crack, she couldn't see any visible progress.

Though outside an early-morning chill still hung in the air, the cabin, which had no ventilation, was hot. Her hair hung over her shoulders and clung to her cheeks as her skin grew damp with perspiration.

"Come on," she urged the stubborn box, pushing with her thumbs until her nails grew white. *"Open!"*

"A penknife might help."

A shadow fell across the doorway, blocking the sunlight that had been streaming onto the box, and Eleanor lifted her head, her heart racing. She had been so absorbed in trying to open the box she had completely forgotten about the ghostly figure that had led her here.

But this was not a ghost. This was Edan, his voice full of his unique blend of amusement and superiority.

She stared, waiting for her heart to slow down. He was backlit by the morning sun and his face was in shadow, but it was obvious that he still wore last night's evening clothes.

So he hadn't been back to his own room all night. Her throat burned, and she had to swallow hard, remembering the sounds she had heard coming from Gina's room.

He probably hadn't slept, and yet he didn't have a hair out of place, not a wrinkle or a smudge on his well-cut tuxedo. How dared he break her heart and not even have the decency to look rumpled?

The tears she had thought were spent suddenly stung her eyes again. But her earlier mantra came to her rescue. He didn't know he had broken her heart. And if she could somehow cap this geyser of pain that had exploded at the sight of him, he never would.

"Penknife?" he repeated, a nudge in his voice as if he were trying to prompt a slow child.

"Unfortunately," she retorted, trying to match his ironic tone, "I don't happen to have a penknife on me."

But he was already holding out his own. He leaned against the doorway, one foot on the top step, the other just inside the cabin, one hand thrust in his pocket. His casual attitude bewildered her, until she realized he didn't know what she held.

"Thank you." Leaning forward, she took the knife. Before she opened it, she looked up at him. "This may be it, you know. It's a Civil War ammunition case, and Captain Wilding's initials are on it." When he didn't respond, she repeated herself, wishing his features weren't obscured by shadows. "This is *it*."

"I assumed it must be," he said smoothly. "What else could drag you out of bed at dawn and have you crawling around in the dust?"

His blasé attitude annoyed her, and she bent her head. Flicking open the penknife, she wedged its silver tip under the box's lid. She had to put all her weight behind it, but finally she felt the metal give. Rust crumbled, raining onto her thighs, as the lid ground open.

Unconsciously she held her breath. She could barely bring herself to look. She had, as a child, so often dreamed of the moment she would open Captain Wilding's treasure box and find...

Well, she never actually saw the treasure in her dreams, but she always awoke from them filled with a happy warmth.

Whatever was in the box in front of her was going to mark the end of a dream and the beginning of reality. Suddenly she wished she'd never found the thing.

Rust clung to her damp palms. Forcing herself to breathe, she looked at Edan, standing in the shadows, and then she looked down at the box. Reality had to be faced.

At first she thought it was just a collection of old papers. Then she distinguished the shape, the numbers, the pictures. Jefferson Davis stared out at her as she slowly unfolded one paper, and she felt her lips part. It was Confederate money. Lots of it—a roll several inches thick.

She rubbed her fingers across the smooth cotton-filled paper. She didn't know how to feel. Disappointed? Perhaps. Today, as a treasure, it was virtually worthless. But as a testimony to Jonathan Wilding's love for Celia Galsworthy, it was touching enough to bring tears to her eyes. It must have been a small fortune in 1860.

She held up the bill for Edan to see, marveling at its good condition. "Money," she said in a voice that sounded as rusty as the hinge on the box. "Confederate money."

"Too bad," he said. "I guess you won't be getting that Lamborghini. Not many dealerships take Confederate money anymore."

She stared at him, disbelieving. How could he sound so smug, so indifferent to the implications of her discovery? He surely hadn't forgotten that Charlotte had promised to leave Wildings to the person who discovered the treasure. She had thought he loved Wildings as much as she did.

Perspiration trickled down her hairline, and she flicked it away with a dirty hand, suddenly seized by an irrational anger. She wanted to smash that sublime confidence, rip away that impenetrable cool facade. She wanted him to *care,* if not about her, then at least about Wildings. She wanted him to feel some of the misery that had been tormenting her ever since she'd heard him in Gina's room.

She gripped the box hard, the rust crumbling under her aching fingers. "Haven't you thought what it means? It means I've won. It means Charlotte will leave Wildings to me."

"It certainly seems that way." He smiled.

It was like talking to a deaf person, like rattling a bolted door. A demon of anger drove her, pushing her to say things she knew were outrageous, trying to break through. "You're taking this awfully well, Edan, considering how thoroughly it's going to mess up all your plans."

"Plans?" He was ominously still, but his tone was calm, measured. "What plans are those?"

"I think you know," she said, aware of the danger signs, but pushing ahead, anyway. At least she knew she had his attention. "Remember Brad Mitchell, the one who wanted to toss you into the Mississippi? Well, he told me all about it last night, all about the rezoning and all about your other hotels.''

She flipped her hair over her shoulder. ''How long did you think you could keep it a secret, Edan? You haven't even told Charlotte, have you?''

He was silent for a moment, as though he didn't trust himself to speak. But she could feel the tension radiating from his body, and somehow his silhouette seemed to grow larger, more ominous, dwarfing the doorway.

''This is certainly a familiar scene,'' he said finally. A cold contempt scored his voice. ''But if I haven't told her, I'm quite sure you'll do it for me, won't you?''

This time she knew she'd reached him. In fact she'd opened the door, broken the bolt and flung it wide. Pandora herself couldn't have let loose more violent emotions. Though Edan didn't move an inch, his hostility emanated into the cabin, filling it, shrinking it to a claustrophobic prison.

''What do you mean?'' Suddenly her throat was dry. She felt as if she had been inhaling dust for a long, long time.

''I mean,'' he said bitterly, ''that we're right back where we started. You with your nasty little nugget of information, eager to run tattling to Charlotte, eager to see how much damage you can do. You haven't changed a bit. It makes me sick.''

She rocked back onto her heels, briefly overwhelmed by the intensity of his words. Had she really wanted to shatter his composure? Had she forgotten what Edan's wrath was like? She felt weak, slightly nauseated. His anger and contempt were blinding, like staring straight into a dying sun.

But she refused to be intimidated.

"I'm not the one who's doing damage here." Her voice was rising. "*You're* the one who's been sneaking around behind Charlotte's back, making plans to do the one thing you know she would absolutely hate. You haven't changed, either, Edan. You're still charming everyone in sight to get what you want. You're still selfish, ambitious, greedy, hypocritical and...and..."

She stumbled on the words, unable to think of the one that would hurt enough. How dared he judge her harshly? He was a user, a taker, a destroyer. He had taken her father's love, her father's business, her place at Wildings, and finally, without remorse, he had taken her innocence. And he had always blamed it all on her. She was on fire with the injustice of it.

But so was he. As her furious words came tumbling out, he lunged through the doorway and grabbed her elbow in a steely grip, yanking her to her feet. His eyes were blazing.

"And now you think you've caught me, don't you? Well, let's go, Eleanor. You can expose me and my diabolical plans." He moved toward the door. "Let's go and tell Charlotte how she's been duped by the devil incarnate."

"No." She resisted, holding on to the doorframe. She wouldn't be pushed around and bullied. "No. Edan, listen. I don't want to tell—"

"Yes." His voice was as unyielding as his hand, and he pulled her relentlessly out of the cabin. She almost tripped on the steps, but he didn't even look back. "We're going to tell her. Right now."

At the foot of the steps, she managed to wrench her arm free. "Listen to me," she insisted, drawing herself up rigidly and standing stock-still. "I don't see any reason to—"

"Just come with me." He obviously wasn't listening to a word she said. He was striding with repressed violence toward the house. He had no intention, clearly, of letting her explain, except in front of Charlotte.

She considered the possibility of ignoring him, of allowing him to go up alone, but she knew he was angry enough to come back, scoop her up and carry her every inch. Hugging her treasure box to her chest, she walked along in his wake with as much dignity as she could muster.

Charlotte was still in bed, of course, and at first she smiled, apparently both surprised and delighted to see them. But she registered the nuances immediately— Edan's stiff silence, Eleanor's flushed defiance, the almost visible wall of anger between them—and her smile faded away.

"What's wrong?" She sat up, propping her pillows behind her, and wrapped a satin bed jacket around her thin shoulders, as though they had brought a frost into the warm room. She leveled a solemn gaze at the two of them. "Edan? Eleanor?" She frowned as the silence lengthened. "What is it?"

Eleanor's chin rose involuntarily. She felt sixteen again, called on the carpet for tattling on Edan and his friends. That was exactly how Edan had wanted her to feel—guilty, frightened and unforgivably at fault.

But it had not been her idea to awaken Charlotte with this mess. Though Edan wouldn't believe it, she had never intended to talk to Charlotte about the zoning at all. She had wanted to talk to *him,* and if he hadn't been so busy romancing every woman in sight she would have done just that.

She shifted her grip on the box and transferred her defiant glare to Edan. Let *him* explain.

He acknowledged her dare with a brief narrowing of his eyes. He seemed to be getting his anger under control, but she knew it still lay there, like an undiluted poison, under the thin coating of civility.

"Eleanor has found out about the rezoning," he said bluntly. Shocked that he should be so direct, Eleanor whipped her gaze back to her grandmother to see how the bombshell affected her. To her astonishment, Charlotte merely nodded.

"And?" Charlotte sounded slightly puzzled.

"And," Edan went on, darting a look toward Eleanor's stunned face, "she suspects me of going behind your back, of secretly plotting the degradation of Wildings by turning it into a two-bit rooming house."

"A two-bit...?" Charlotte laughed. "Well, hardly!" She turned to Eleanor, her puzzled frown still in place. "Why would you think that, Eleanor? Don't you know what a fine reputation the other Wilding hotel properties have?"

Shock, humiliation and a furious resentment seemed to have robbed Eleanor of her voice, and she couldn't answer. She stared at Edan. It had been a setup. He'd dragged her up here just to show Charlotte what a nasty little talebearer she was. And Charlotte wasn't horrified. She wasn't even surprised. She had known all along.

"You knew?" The words were a non sequitur, but Charlotte clearly understood.

"Of course," she said mildly.

"Of course she knew," Edan echoed, though his tone was far from mild. "Why wouldn't she know? You're the only stranger here, Eleanor."

Before Eleanor could recover from that breathtaking punch, he turned to Charlotte. "Eleanor probably didn't even know Wildings Realty owned hotels.'' His face was grim, his eyes accusing. ''All the corporate reports we sent her have been returned to my office, unopened.''

Charlotte frowned at Eleanor, a sadness clouding her eyes. ''Really, Eleanor? But why? It's half your company, too.''

And then Eleanor knew she *had* to find words. Even if it would do no good, she had to try to defend herself. She had believed that Charlotte had understood. It was horrible to realize she hadn't—like a drowning man discovering that his lifeline had been severed.

''But the company isn't mine, not really,'' she said urgently. How could she make Charlotte understand? ''Father left it to Edan. I have absolutely no legal right to make any decisions, not even to give advice. Edan doesn't need my approval to buy anything from a doghouse to the Taj Mahal.''

''Technically that's true of course.'' Charlotte seemed to recognize the distinction, but to find it relatively unimportant. ''But he did leave you fifty percent of all the net profits. That should have given you some interest in what was happening.''

''Well, it didn't. What it gave me was the determination to build a life for myself.'' Eleanor tried not to let her voice get out of control, but it had taken her a long time to come to terms with her father's death and his decisions regarding the company. Frank would say, of course, that she never had come to terms with it; otherwise, it wouldn't be this difficult to explain now.

In spite of her efforts, her voice broke. ''Don't you see, Gran? It was too late to hope for his love or his respect, and I didn't need his charity.''

"You're a fool, Eleanor." Edan broke in, his voice rough with disdain. "Why the hell do you think I was sending you those reports? You're right—I didn't have to do it. I sent them because I knew your father had made a mistake, and I wanted to correct it as best I could. I wanted you to be involved. If you hadn't been so set on being such a pouting brat, I would have *given* you half of the legal rights."

That hurt. It hurt so much she was afraid she wouldn't be able to stand up. She turned to him with all her bitter misery in her eyes and in her voice.

"Sorry," she said acidly. "I guess I wasn't interested in *your* charity, either."

She thought for a moment he might hit her. His eyes grew as black as midnight, and his hands balled into fists at his side. Somehow, though, he checked himself and turned slowly, rigidly, to Charlotte.

"This is pointless," he said, his jaw so tight his words were clipped and mechanical. "I have work to do in Vicksburg. I won't be back for several weeks." Without looking at Eleanor, he grabbed her arm and held it up, showing Charlotte the box. "Eleanor found the treasure this morning."

Charlotte sat up straighter, her wide eyes darting to the box Eleanor held. "You mean there really was one?"

He nodded curtly. "I want you to stand by your word, Charlotte, and make her the sole beneficiary in your will." His face grew even darker. "Leave her *everything,* do you understand? Every penny, every strip of wallpaper, every twig on every tree."

"No, Edan." Charlotte's face looked suddenly very old, and she held out her frail hands to him. "You know I had always hoped that the two of you—"

"I know," he said, and his voice suddenly softened, as though he could not bear the pain he heard in her voice. Ignoring Eleanor, he walked over to the bed and put his hand in Charlotte's. "But it won't work, Charley. It isn't ever going to happen. Now get Evanston out here and make him rewrite your will."

As Charlotte opened her mouth with a short sound of protest, he nudged her cheek with the back of his hand. "All of it, Charley. I fully expect you to be with us for another fifty years, but Nell needs to know it's settled."

He smiled finally, but it was a short smile with as much bitterness in it as mirth. "And since Nell can't dirty her hands with Wildings Realty money, she's going to need to sell some of the stocks to pay inheritance taxes. Somehow I don't think a treasure of ten thousand Confederate dollars is going to carry much weight with the federal government."

Obviously not paying any attention to what he was saying, Charlotte clutched at his hand, as though the force of her desire alone could keep him from leaving. But he was too strong. He squeezed her hand, kissed her cheek and headed for the door.

But Eleanor had heard him, had heard every amazing word, and a disagreeable realization crept into her mind.

"Ten thousand Confederate dollars?" she asked numbly as he passed near her, leaning up against the wall to brace herself for his answer. "How do you know how many Confederate dollars are in the box?"

Clutching the box to her chest like a frightened child holding a security blanket, she made herself meet his eyes, though the room was whirling weirdly around her and a dull roar was assaulting her ears.

"How do you know exactly what's in this box?" she demanded in a stranger's high tight voice.

"I know," he said with a grim smile, "because five years ago, while you were busy sulking in the California sun, I found it."

CHAPTER ELEVEN

Two weeks later, Eleanor sat on the side of Charlotte's bed, struggling with the strange collection of vowels and syllables of Tolstoy's people and places: Dmitrievna, Vasilyevna, Ilarionovitch ... ugh! With relief she noticed that her grandmother's eyes were closed and, pulling the grosgrain bookmark into place, she slid *War and Peace* onto the nightstand with a sigh.

In silence she watched Charlotte sleeping. Her struggle with Tolstoy over, Eleanor knew she had to face the other, far more disturbing struggle that was taking place in her heart.

For two full weeks she had managed to avoid it. That first day had been pure hell, enduring the wild and exuberant family celebration over the finding of the treasure. And then she'd had to say goodbye to everyone. A subdued Gina had seemed abnormally quiet as she took her leave, which didn't surprise Eleanor since Edan was already gone, apparently without saying goodbye to Gina at all.

Saying goodbye to Kelly was the hardest. She had grown to care greatly for the girl and she knew she would miss her. But Kelly promised to write, and she drove off happily with her parents, who, for once, seemed to be on good terms.

Finally everyone was gone. Eleanor put the treasure box on her dresser and concentrated on devoting herself to Charlotte.

She prepared meals, drew baths, changed linens, chauffeured for outings, administered medicines, conferred with doctors. She lost long hard-fought games of Scrabble, browsed for hours through musty scrapbooks and giggled far into the night over silly jokes. She even, in an excess of loyalty, ploughed through *War and Peace*.

The only thing she refused to do was talk about Edan. She wasn't ready, and Charlotte seemed to accept that. They both skirted the issue, walking carefully around it, as if it was a conversational sinkhole.

He called sometimes, she knew, because she would find Charlotte sitting up in bed with her face lit by that special glow she reserved for him. But he never asked to speak to Eleanor, and he never came to Wildings. The implication was clear. He would return if, and only if, Eleanor left.

She stood up abruptly, the bed creaking at the sudden shift, and wandered out to the porch. The mist was thin tonight, just tired wisps of gray that littered the yard.

She leaned her head against the pillar. It was shocking, really, how much she missed Edan. Wildings wasn't the same without him. The place was diminished somehow, smaller and dimmer and less glamorous. That was nonsense, of course. She smiled tiredly at her foolishness—did she truly think that even the mist didn't have the heart to be robust in his absence? Whatever the real reason, even the treasure box sat untouched on her dresser, looking like merely a bit of moldy metal.

She slept fitfully, too, her body uncomfortable with the new sensuality it couldn't conveniently discard simply because he was gone. She tossed with a restless energy, dreamed beautiful dreams of mist and midnight, and awakened tired and aching.

But she didn't call him. She picked up the telephone a thousand times, only to lay it quietly in its cradle again, undialed. Each time the image of his cold face rose up and stopped her. She couldn't bring herself to beg him to come home.

Until today.

Today her pride finally seemed unimportant, a triviality compared to the tragedy that might be on its way. And she wouldn't be begging—at least not for herself.

It would be for Charlotte. Charlotte whose health seemed to be failing, and who had already survived two strokes but might not survive another.

It had been only little things, really. Eleanor frowned, trying to sum up the signs that had set her nerves tingling with this terrible premonition. Charlotte had been confused at dinner, thinking Edan would be joining them. Realizing her mistake, she had laughed the incident off, but then, on her way upstairs, she had swayed slightly on the last step, as though a dizzy spell had come on suddenly. And, finally, she had complained of a headache as she settled into bed.

Not much to go on—but Eleanor's instincts told her something was wrong. She gripped the balustrade and stared, unseeing, down at the mist. She didn't want to believe it. Her whole heart recoiled. But the doctor had said another stroke could happen at any time, with or without warning.

And Edan would want to be here.

She knew it, without a moment's doubt. She knew too well how he must be feeling. Out there, cut off, not knowing how things stood, not knowing whether something dreadful might happen while he was gone. She could hardly bear to think of it. Even though he had chosen to leave, she knew he must be riddled with anxiety, paralyzed with worry. She couldn't, just couldn't, let anything happen without calling him.

And so pride be damned. She would do it.

He had a house of his own here in town. She found the telephone number in Charlotte's address book. When, after the fourth ring, his answering machine picked up, Eleanor was confused. It was almost midnight, and she had naively expected him to be at home.

"Edan," she began awkwardly, "it's Eleanor. I'm calling about Gran." But that might alarm him, so she hurried on. "She's okay, really, don't worry. It's just that..." Well, what was it? A headache? Suddenly pride became an issue again. This sounded so stupid he'd probably conclude that she was inventing excuses to call him.

"It's just that I'm a little worried about her." Eleanor rolled her eyes. Hadn't she just told him not to be? "She's had a headache and some dizziness. Little things. But I thought..." She stopped and tried to think of something intelligent to say. "I thought you'd like to know."

On that brilliant note she hung up. She checked in on Charlotte one more time and, pleased to see her sleeping quietly, the white comforter rising and falling with peaceful regularity, she went to her own bed.

As though making the call to Edan had somehow relieved her mind, she slept well and she slept late. Charlotte must have risen first and gone into the bathroom to start her own toilette, because Eleanor was still in bed when she heard the awful sounds. A cry, a fall, and then the most awful sound of all. The sound of silence.

BY TEN O'CLOCK, Eleanor had been pacing the front walk for an hour, grinding the wisteria to a sticky mush beneath her feet. Dr. Parker was upstairs with Charlotte, doing his best to persuade her to go to the hospital for tests, and Eleanor had left at least a thousand incoherent messages on Edan's answering machine.

Where was he? She tried to breathe deeply, but coughed on the cloying sweetness of the mangled wisteria. Where was he?

She sank onto the wrought-iron bench, trying to think clearly. She had called the realty office, but they didn't know where he was, either. They thought he was in Vicksburg. She had called the Wildings hotel in Vicksburg, but he had left yesterday. Desperate, she had called his mother at her resort hotel in California, but even she hadn't known where to find Edan. She dug her fingers into the cold iron filigree. Where was he?

And when she thought she could stand it no longer, miraculously he was there, striding up the walk toward her. For the first time that she could remember, he was disheveled, his hair tousled, his white cotton shirt a maze of wrinkles. He looked very tired.

Yet to her he couldn't have looked more wonderful. "Oh, Edan. Thank heavens." Running up to him, she took his shirt in both hands. A few more wrinkles wouldn't matter. "You're here."

His face was rigid and, up this close, she could see how shadowed his eyes were. "I got your message about three this morning," he said, "when I called home to check my machine. I've been driving all night. Is she really okay?''

Eleanor, her hands still tangled in his shirt, was confused. Last night? He must have heard only her first message. That meant he didn't know Charlotte had had another stroke.

''No,'' she said. ''I mean yes. We don't really know yet. She seems fine. But I don't know— The doctor said—''

He took her hands in his, cutting off her stream of half sentences with a firm grip. ''Nell. What are you talking about?''

Her eyes searched his face miserably, wishing she didn't have to tell him this. He looked too tired to take it. ''She had another stroke, Edan. This morning. She fell in the bathroom. The doctor is with her right now.''

For a moment she thought he was angry. His jaw clenched and a small pulse jerked in his temple. ''I'm sorry,'' she began, ''I should have called you sooner. . . .''

But he wasn't listening. He was already halfway to the front door. He moved so fast his feet didn't seem to touch the ground, an illusion enhanced by the muffling effect of the wet carpet of wisteria. Then, as she hurried helplessly in his wake, he took the steps two at a time and disappeared into the house.

She caught up with him at the door to Charlotte's room. He knocked sharply and flung the door open. He crossed the wide room in three steps and knelt on one knee at Charlotte's side.

''I'm glad you're here, Bond,'' Dr. Parker said without looking up from the hieroglyphics he was scribbling on a prescription form. ''Tell this stubborn old woman she *must* go to the hospital. She's being impossible. I can't do a thing with her."

Edan gave Charlotte a grin and slipped her hand between his two larger ones. "I don't think I can help you, Doc," he said, and though his voice held a teasing note it was strangely husky. "I haven't been able to make her do a single thing she didn't want to do in the past ten years."

"That's right," Charlotte said testily, although she was grinning at Edan. "Neither one of you scamps is going to bully me into anything. I know what's wrong with me. I've had another blasted stroke, and I don't need your fancy tests to tell me so, Roger." The doctor looked offended, but she tsked at the sight of his disapproving frown. "Well, it's true. You'll just cart me off to your precious hospital, X-ray every inch of me, scratch your chin, and then come and tell me I've had a stroke."

Edan chuckled, though the doctor's frown hadn't lightened one bit. "Sassy old rascal, isn't she?"

"Charlotte Wilding," Dr. Parker said, glaring sternly over his half glasses, "you need a CAT scan. How are we going to determine the extent of the damage—"

"The old-fashioned way." She used her right hand to cover her eyes, as if such stupidity exhausted her. "If I can't move my left arm, we're going to assume that my left side was damaged. If I can't do multiplication tables, we'll assume that my brain was damaged. If I can't endure the puffed-up pontifications of swaggers like you—"

"Then we'll assume," Edan broke in, "that part of you is quite normal."

Charlotte chuckled, too, recognizing an ally. "So go away, Roger. I've got my children to take care of me."

She embraced both Edan and Eleanor with her warm smile. "I don't know if I'm going to live twenty minutes or twenty years, but I'm going to spend every second of it here at Wildings."

A tear she hadn't known was there tickled Eleanor's mouth and pooled between her closed lips. She licked the salty warmth away and tried to smile.

"Gran..." she began slowly. She understood how Charlotte felt, but it frightened her that her grandmother refused to go to the hospital. Maybe there was something Dr. Parker could do, something that could keep this from happening again.

"Don't you start, too," Charlotte said waspishly, though her eyes were tender. "You show Dr. Parker down to his car. I want to talk to Edan alone." As Eleanor hesitated, she groaned. "If I wasn't stuck in this bed, you people wouldn't dare be so impertinent. Go now, and take this bossy medicine man with you."

Dr. Parker flipped his case shut with a disgusted snap, rolled his eyes and took Eleanor's arm. "Let's go, Eleanor," he said, but his tone was not as indignant as he might have liked. It was clear he had a soft spot for impossible old ladies. "Don't think this is the end of it, Charlotte. I'll get you in that hospital if it's the last thing I do."

"Don't bet your little black bag on it, Roger," Charlotte called as the door closed behind them.

Eleanor started to apologize, but Dr. Parker just chuckled, a mixture of amusement and resignation, and put his arm around her shoulders as they went down the wide stairs together.

"She was that way in high school, and she'll be that way when she knocks on the pearly gates and tells St. Peter the damn place isn't up to Wildings standards.

And that may not be for a while yet," he added, squeezing Eleanor's shoulders as if he had felt the trembling she was trying to control. "She's such a tough old bird St. Peter may just decide he doesn't want her."

She appreciated his effort, but dread had settled like a cold lump in her stomach and no joke could make it go away.

"Dr. Parker," she asked, "what can we expect? Will she—"

He stopped her midsentence, dropping his whimsical tone. "Seriously, Eleanor, there's no way of predicting these things, but my best guess is that she'll be fine. None of these strokes was massive. Some people have them and don't even know it. She could have several more little ones, or never have one again."

He smiled at her over his glasses. "Basically she's as strong as an ox. And with you and Edan both here, she's happy, which is the best medicine on the planet."

Tossing his bag onto the seat, he climbed into his expensive sedan. "In fact, I'd bet my life savings that she'll be here to boss around the next generation of Wildings, too."

Eleanor gave him a grateful smile and waved as he pulled slowly out of the drive. His words, which had the ring of sincerity, had helped. Pocketing the prescriptions he had given her, she walked slowly across the lawn to the gazebo.

From there she could see Charlotte's window. Surely her grandmother would send Edan down to get her when she was ready. She didn't want to interrupt their time alone.

She sat on the stone bench and stared at the white muslin curtains that hung there, for the moment content just to be here at Wildings. Content to watch the white billowing clouds pile up in the sky over Wildings' gabled roof, content to know that Edan and Charlotte were safe within its walls.

It wouldn't last forever. She knew that. Soon she would have to talk to Edan, and the cease-fire between them would be shattered. She'd have to bring up the subject of Wildings. The whole treasure hunt had been nonsense. Wildings should go to the people who loved it best, not to the people who could best afford it.

She closed her eyes, unwilling to deal with the dilemma now. Tomorrow would be time enough. Tomorrow, which was already traveling toward them, a shadow on the other side of the earth.

As if she had summoned it, a shadow fell across her, robbing her of the sun's warmth. She opened her eyes and saw Edan standing there.

"Is she...?"

"She's sleeping." Edan said the words wearily and, putting one foot up on the bench, rested his elbow on his knee and rubbed his eyes. "Parker gave her a sedative. She should sleep most of the day."

He let his hands fall, and looked at Eleanor through dark and hooded eyes. "We need to talk."

A pang of disappointment stabbed through her. Not yet. Couldn't she hold on to this fragile peace a little longer? Tomorrow would be soon enough.... But she could tell by the flat tone of his voice that he could not be put off.

"All right," she said obediently, and waited.

He looked away, across the grounds toward the house, just as she had done earlier. In the high noon sun, the house sparkled, pristinely white. She wondered whether it seemed as achingly beautiful to him as it did to her.

"We have to work things out, Nell." He didn't look at her. "For Charlotte's sake. We have to."

"I know." She threaded her fingers together and stared at them. "I've already been thinking about it. There must be some way we can share Wildings, Edan. It's ridiculous to think you wouldn't inherit it equally. Surely we can work something out—"

"Not Wildings, damn it!" He wheeled to face her, and his dark eyes were angry, his body tense. "This isn't about Wildings. It's just a house, don't you know that yet? It's us she cares about. *Us!*"

She frowned, caught unawares. "What do you mean?"

He swore under his breath. "I mean she hates to see us always arguing. She's afraid we're going to go through life making each other miserable."

Eleanor smiled grimly. "Well, that's certainly been our pattern, hasn't it?"

He nodded. "But for her sake we need to try to break the pattern. I've been thinking a lot about us. Have you?"

"Not really." She couldn't admit it, not when she remembered the way they had left things. He had been so disdainful, so cutting. "I didn't even know there *was* an us."

"Damn it, Nell!" The words exploded from him. "Can't we get past all this bickering for once?" He gestured toward the house. "Doesn't Charlotte's stroke change your perspective at all? Doesn't it seem bigger than our petty arguments?"

She flushed, chastened. She knew exactly what he meant. In the presence of Charlotte's courage, it seemed absurd not to be honest with him. "Yes," she said meekly. "It does."

"Okay. Then let's try to sort this out. Be straight with each other, for once in our lives. Can't you do that?"

She shivered, in spite of the sun. Could she? Could she be honest enough to tell him how much she had always loved him, and how that thwarted love had made her do such stupid things—made her seduce him here in this gazebo, made her try to ruin his friendship with her father and, finally, made her run away? She didn't answer him.

"Well, I can." He sat on the bench opposite her and leaned forward. The sleeves of his white shirt were rolled up, exposing lean muscular forearms. The sun glistened on the dark hair that dusted them. "Over the past two weeks, I've thought of at least a million mistakes I've made with you. Let's start there. Let me tell you where I think I'm to blame."

She stared, unable to respond intelligently. He thought they *shared* the blame? This was certainly a novel approach. Arranging her face in a noncommittal expression, she hugged her elbows and listened.

"Okay. From the beginning, then. When my mother married your father, I was going through some tough times." He spoke slowly, not meeting her eyes. "My own father had left us when I was six. That's hard on kids—at that age they're pretty egocentric. They tend to blame themselves for everything."

She nodded. It was true. She saw it often at the center.

"Anyhow, Dad just disappeared. He didn't write, didn't call, didn't visit, didn't seem to give a damn what happened to his only son. So when your father came on the scene and seemed to think I was so wonderful..."

He got to his feet, apparently too restless to sit. As he stood at the arched opening, the sun cast checkered shadows through the lattice onto his shirt.

"Well, I couldn't get enough of it. I needed to have a father to look up to, a father to make me feel wanted." He turned, meeting her gaze squarely. "So I took yours."

She fidgeted, making a small sound of protest. She hadn't expected this . . . this naked honesty.

"Yes, I did." He wouldn't allow her to contradict him. "I see that now. It was damned selfish of me. But I didn't understand how important a father's love is to a daughter. I was too wrapped up in my own needs to think about yours."

"I've realized that about myself, as well," she managed to say. Her voice sounded unused and squeaky. "You seemed so confident. I never even considered the possibility that you were hurting under all that macho perfection."

He smiled, just a little. "That was the idea. I didn't want anyone to know. But that probably wasn't even the worst of it. The worst of it was that the perfect stepson was fool enough to fall in love with his little 'sister.'"

She gasped, and her hands clenched tightly, the knuckles whitening. Love? She'd never heard him say the word, couldn't believe she was hearing it now. Her heart was beating so fast it was as if something small and wild was trapped in her chest.

"You were such a fascinating little person. I'd never seen anyone quite like you. You were so alive, such a quixotic mixture of spunk and vulnerability, of bravado and need. You were a dreamer and a fighter, the softest, most intuitive soul I'd ever met inside the bossiest tomboy exterior I'd ever seen. Everything you did, you put your heart into. You hated fiercely. And you loved fiercely.''

He grabbed the lattice, just as he had that night long ago, exerting so much pressure the wood creaked. ''I was so ashamed, Nell. You can't imagine. After the night we . . . out here . . .'' He looked around the gazebo with dark eyes, as though he could see it all happening again. ''I had let your father down. But most of all I had let you down. I was supposed to be the adult.''

That was unfair. She couldn't let it pass. ''But I forced you,'' she said, though the embarrassment of admitting it burned at her cheeks. ''I made it impossible for you to say no.''

He looked up at that, his eyes squinted against the sun.

''Nell,'' he said, his voice soft, ''it's never impossible to say no. I could have stopped. I should have. But I had wanted you for so long . . .''

He turned away again and went on, ''After that night I couldn't even trust myself around you, couldn't trust myself not to do it all over again. God, what a mess! The perfect brother couldn't think about anything but making wild love to his sixteen-year-old stepsister.'' He lowered his head and groaned, as though even the memory hurt.

She half rose from her seat, tortured by the pain she heard in his voice. ''But I wanted you, too, Edan. I came to you, over and over, and you acted as if you hated me. You sent me away. . . .''

''I hated myself.'' He didn't look at her. ''Not you. Myself. There I was, in a hell of shame and regret, and all I wanted was to tear your clothes off and make you mine again. I wanted to feel you, to smell you, to touch you. I wanted . . . until I thought I'd go mad from it."

"Edan, I—"

"No. Let me finish. While you were away at school, I even allowed myself to build this incredible fantasy that you loved me, too. I began to imagine that maybe later, when you were a little older, we could . . ." His voice changed. Bitterness gave it a sharp edge. "But then you came home, and I saw how stupid those delusions had been. You were so full of resentment. There was that stunt with Tony that was clearly intended to hurt me. . . ."

He stopped, as though he had come to the end of his recitation. "And then you ran away as soon as you were out of school. When you came back for your father's funeral, you were still full of hatred—"

"I did hate you then!" she cried, the need to defend herself shooting the words out of her. "You should have called me. You should have told me Father was sick. Didn't you know how it would feel, having him die before he and I had made up?" She felt tears at the back of her throat and finished on a weak listless note. "You should have called."

"I tried to make him tell you." Edan's voice was tired now, too, as though the weight of all the guilt and anger had exhausted his energy. "But he thought you were too troubled. He thought you didn't need anything else to worry about."

She tried to be reasonable, to fight down the pain that even now arose at the memory. "I suppose I asked for that, behaving the way I did. But it hurt, Edan. It hurt so much. That was why I refused to take the money from the business. Not because he had left it to you, but because he hadn't cared enough to want to see me before he died."

Edan's eyes softened. "He didn't think he was going to die, Nellie. He wouldn't accept how serious his condition was. If he had, I think he would have called you."

Though her tears were too close to the surface to permit speech, Eleanor nodded, accepting the truth of what he said. Her father had been like that, powerful, indomitable. She could imagine him refusing to acknowledge that death could defeat him.

Slowly, as she tried to get her emotions back under control, Edan came closer and, with a finger under her chin, tilted her face toward his. "I probably should have called you, anyway," he admitted. "But things were such a mess between us..."

"I know," she whispered. "I really do know."

"But you surprised me this time, Nellie. You didn't take advantage of your chance to pay me back for all of that." He raised one brow. "You called me. Even before Charlotte had the stroke, you had already called to warn me."

Her eyes widened. "Did you really think I wouldn't?"

His dark gray eyes searched her face, as if she were a puzzle he couldn't solve. "I don't know what to think, Nellie. When we're together, there is something... something real and wonderful between us. You try, but you can't quite hide it."

She lowered her eyes, but he nudged her chin, and she opened them again. "But then it's gone," he said, "and something wild and bitter takes its place. Like that day in the cabin, when you found the treasure. You were so full of hate that day."

She shut her eyes again, desperate to escape his probing gaze. She could tell the truth, but only if she didn't have to look into his eyes. "I...heard you in Gina's room. I was looking for you, so that we could talk about the zoning. You were in her room. She was...it was obvious that you..." She turned her head, overcome with remembered pain and embarrassment.

"It was the same *day,* Edan," she said to the wall. "The same day you'd made love to me. And there you were, in her room, and she was moaning...."

She couldn't finish. Her throat was impassable. But it didn't matter, because, amazingly, he was laughing.

"Gina was..." His laughter grew. "Oh, my poor Nellie, what a dirty mind you have! Did you think Gina was moaning in rapture because I was busy making passionate love to her?"

She blushed and frowned at him. Of course that was what she'd thought. Why was that so funny?

"Oh, if only you had confronted us then and there, Nell." He touched the blush, on both cheeks, with his thumbs. "You'd have seen a pretty picture. The lovely Gina was disgracing herself, having consumed who knows how many glasses of champagne at the party. And I was holding the bowl."

The image didn't sink in for a moment, but when it did, a bubble of laughter rose in her throat, dissolving the lingering tightness of tears.

"Gina was...?" She began to chuckle. "You mean she was..."

"I mean she was being violently, disgustingly sick. Making love to her would have been a physical impossibility, even if I'd wanted to." He tilted his head, smiling. "Which I didn't."

She wasn't laughing anymore. Her eyes were fixed on the hard line of his lips. ''What I wanted,'' he said, his lips moving sensuously, ''was to make love to you.''

A shaking started in her midsection, and it spread down her legs and up into her chest. But she had more to say, and she hurried to say it for fear the shaking would take over.

''I wasn't going to take the zoning story to Charlotte,'' she said desperately. ''You have to believe that.'

He smiled. ''And I wasn't going to turn Wildings into a hotel. Charlotte and I arranged to get the variance because we didn't see how you were going to afford Wildings by yourself. It looked more and more as if you would never accept my help.''

No wonder he had been furious! To have his good intentions thrown into his face like sins. ''I was looking for you so that I could ask *you*,'' she said, praying he would believe her. ''I knew you thought that I was a tattletale, but it was just that my father thought you could do no wrong—''

''Shh.'' He hushed her words, which had begun to tumble over each other. ''I know that. And you were right to resent it. I should have been more sensitive to what you needed.''

He sounded so tender, like the Edan of her dreams. ''While we're confessing, I should tell you about this.'' He put his hand in his shirt pocket. ''I stole part of Captain Wilding's treasure. It was rolled up inside the bills.'' He held his hand out, palm open.

With trembling fingers she reached for the object that lay there sparkling in the sun. It was small for a treasure—so small. A tiny gold circlet. A beautiful wedding ring.

Speechless, she picked it up. It was engraved, with old-fashioned lettering: "To CG from JW, 1865."

In her mind, she filled out the initials: To Celia Galsworthy from Jonathan Wilding. And then she couldn't read anything at all; her eyes were full of tears.

"They were married," she whispered. "He did marry her."

Edan gathered Eleanor into his arms. "Of course he did. He loved her." He rubbed his lips across the top of her head. "And besides, they'd probably already misbehaved here in the gazebo. He had to make an honest woman out of her. I can understand that. I plan to do it myself."

She folded her hand around the ring and pressed her fist against her heart. She still couldn't quite believe it.

"I put the treasure back so that you could officially find it," he said, his voice low and teasing. "But I thought I'd better keep the ring in case someone beat you to it."

She squeezed the ring harder, assuring herself of its reality. "It's amazing, really, that I did find it. It was so strange, Edan. I saw a man's shape in the mist . . ."

"Just a gray and ghostly form?" He finished the sentence for her, his voice rich with a theatrical melodrama. "Floating through the mist at dawn? And it led you straight to the cabin?"

She pulled back and looked into his smiling eyes accusingly.

"You didn't." His grin deepened, and she slapped her palm against his broad chest. "Edan Bond, you didn't!"

"Well, I'd waited as long as I could for you to find it," he said in a hotly defensive and utterly artificial tone. He grinned again, deep dimples notching his cheeks. "But for a lady who pretends to be psychic, you can be unbelievably dense. You and Kelly must have been practically sitting on top of the fool thing, and you still couldn't find it. Time was running out." He dipped his voice to spectral levels and ran his hands like ghostly fingers up her back. "It called for drastic measures."

"Hey," she said, the word coming out on an erratic burst of air. Her lungs, like every other part of her body, seemed to be tightening into a maddening, thrilling coil. "I haven't listed *my* sins yet."

He moved his hands languidly down her back. "Unless they're sins of lust, I haven't the slightest interest in them."

It made sense to her. His fingers were chasing a stampede of shivers across her shoulder blades. They raced around her arms and collected on the tips of her breasts. Reveling in the exquisite sensations, she pressed herself into his chest and wrapped her arms around him.

She looked around her, at the bench, at the purple wisteria that littered the floor, at the oak branches that filtered the sun above them. She looked at every familiar inch of the gazebo that had witnessed the birth of their love, and she smiled, lifting her face to seek his lips.

When he kissed her, the tenderness took her breath away. She hadn't realized he was capable of such sweetness—or how arousing such a gentle kiss could be. Before he lifted his head, she was melting, like ice in the Mississippi sun.

"Funny," she whispered, "you don't feel like a ghost."

"This is nothing," he said, lowering his lips to her neck. "You'll be surprised how corporeal I can be."

She smiled. "Actually I remember quite well. It was right here, and it was midnight, and you didn't want to touch me . . ."

He gripped her upper arms. "Yes, I did, you tormenting creature, and you know it." He resumed his attentions to her neck. "Besides, I thought we decided that we can stop dredging up those old sins."

She felt slightly light-headed, as though his words were banishing the thick clouds that had hung over her for as long as she could remember.

"I don't know," she said, her voice wobbly and uncertain. "Someone once said there was no statute of limitations on the sins of youth."

"Well, I refuse to pay for mine anymore." He tunneled his fingers sensuously into her hair. "I absolutely refuse to feel guilty every time we make love out here."

She drew back, pretending indignation. "What makes you think we're going to do that?"

But he didn't fall for it, even for an instant. "Because this is where I found my treasure."

"No, you didn't." She frowned at him. "It was in the slave cabin. I hope we're not going to have to go *there* to commemorate the occasion."

"That was just money." He lowered her to the floor, where her hair spread out against a pillow of silken wisteria. "The treasure I was looking for is right here in my arms."

Take 4 bestselling love stories FREE

Plus get a FREE surprise gift!

HARLEQUIN
·HISTORICAL·

CHRISTMAS

·STORIES·1992·

**Capture the magic and romance of Christmas in the 1800s
with HARLEQUIN HISTORICAL CHRISTMAS STORIES
1992, a collection of three stories by celebrated historical
authors. The perfect Christmas gift!**

**Don't miss these heartwarming stories, available in
November wherever Harlequin books are sold:**

**MISS MONTRACHET REQUESTS by Maura Seger
CHRISTMAS BOUNTY by Erin Yorke
A PROMISE KEPT by Bronwyn Williams**

**Plus, as an added bonus, you can receive a FREE keepsake
Christmas ornament. Just collect four proofs of purchase
from any November or December 1992 Harlequin or
Silhouette series novels, or from any Harlequin or
Silhouette Christmas collection, and receive a beautiful
dated brass Christmas candle ornament.**

Mail this certificate along with four (4) proof-of-purchase coupons plus $1.50 postage and
handling (check or money order—do not send cash), payable to Harlequin Books, to: **In the
U.S.:** P.O. Box 9057, Buffalo, NY 14269-9057; **In Canada:** P.O. Box 622, Fort Erie, Ontario,
L2A 5X3.

ONE PROOF OF PURCHASE	Name: _____
	_____
	Address: _____
	_____
	City: _____
	State/Province: _____
	Zip/Postal Code: _____

HX92POP   093 KAG